T0343566

Don't think there are no second chances.
Life always offers you a second chance...
It's called tomorrow.

—NICHOLAS SPARKS, *THE NOTEBOOK*

MYSTERIES OF COBBLE HILL FARM

MYSTERIES OF COBBLE HILL FARM

Caught in
a Trap

BETH ADAMS

A Gift from Guideposts

Thank you for your purchase! We want to express our gratitude for your support with a special gift just for you.

Dive into **Spirit Lifters**, a complimentary e-book that will fortify your faith, offering solace during challenging moments. Its 31 carefully selected scripture verses will soothe and uplift your soul.

Please use the QR code or go to **guideposts.org/ spiritlifters** to download.

Mysteries of Cobble Hill Farm is a trademark of Guideposts.

Published by Guideposts
100 Reserve Road, Suite E200, Danbury, CT 06810
Guideposts.org

This is a work of fiction. While the setting of Mysteries of Cobble Hill Farm as presented in this series is fictional, the location of Yorkshire, England, actually exists, and some places and characters may be based on actual places and people whose identities have been used with permission or fictionalized to protect their privacy. Apart from the actual people, events, and locales that figure into the fiction narrative, all other names, characters, businesses, and events are the creation of the author's imagination and any resemblance to actual persons or events is coincidental. Every attempt has been made to credit the sources of copyrighted material used in this book. If any such acknowledgment has been inadvertently omitted or miscredited, receipt of such information would be appreciated.

Scripture references are from the following sources: *The Holy Bible, King James Version* (KJV). *The Holy Bible, New International Version* (NIV). Copyright © 1973, 1978, 1984, 2011 by Biblica, Inc. Used by permission of Zondervan. All rights reserved worldwide. www.zondervan.com.

Cover and interior design by Müllerhaus
Cover illustration by Bob Kayganich at Illustration Online LLC.
Typeset by Aptara, Inc.

ISBN 978-1-961442-13-9 (hardcover)
ISBN 978-1-961442-14-6 (softcover)
ISBN 978-1-961442-15-3 (epub)

Printed and bound in the United States of America
$PrintCode

MYSTERIES OF COBBLE HILL FARM

Caught in
a Trap

GLOSSARY OF UK TERMS

boot • trunk

cheeky • charmingly impudent

chips • fries

chockablock • very busy

football • soccer

mate • friend

sacked • fired

trolley • grocery cart

wellies • Wellington rubber boots

CHAPTER ONE

Harriet Bailey patted Hercules, the young Portuguese water dog who'd gotten sick after eating some of Madison Tyler's leftover Easter chocolate, before she headed for the door.

"He'll be back to normal soon," Harriet promised Meredith, Madison's mother.

Meredith pressed her lips together then said, "I'll make sure the rest of the candy is where he can't get into it. I didn't realize Madison had put it on the bottom shelf." She stroked the dog's head, and he leaned against her.

"These things happen," Harriet said. "He's still a puppy, so he's going to get into everything. You did the right thing by bringing him in."

"Thank you, Harriet. I appreciate your kindness." Meredith's tired face betrayed the smallest hint of a smile. "You're just like your grandfather that way."

Harriet thanked her and walked out into the hall, smiling. She couldn't think of a better compliment than being compared to her grandfather, Harold Bailey, who had run the clinic before her. Now she made her way up front and saw that the waiting room was empty except for her receptionist and friend, Polly Thatcher.

"Was Hercules the last one for the day?" Harriet was scheduled to have dinner with Will Knight, the minister of White Church. They'd been steadily dating for a few months, and she was eager to get going.

"Er—sort of." Polly tugged at a loose thread on the cuff of her sweater.

"What do you mean, 'sort of'?"

"It's a bit strange," Polly said. "We just got a phone call from Van. He's at the marina in Whitby."

"Okay." That didn't seem so strange. Van Worthington was a detective constable with the local police force, and he was dating Polly. After a brief period apart, they were back together, deliriously happy, and talking constantly. A call from him wasn't exactly out of the ordinary.

"He asked if you could come down to the marina. I guess there's a lobster he wants you to take a look at."

"A lobster?" She couldn't have heard that right. Harriet treated all kinds of animals in her practice, from cows and horses to dogs and cats—even the occasional camel, zebra, and iguana. But she'd never been called to care for a lobster. She'd never even heard of a vet being called to care for a lobster.

"That's what he said. Apparently, there's a 'lobster in distress.' He's asking if you can come help them with it."

"What does that mean? How can you tell if a lobster is in distress?" Harriet knew nothing about lobster diseases.

"I have no idea," Polly admitted. "What should I tell him?"

"Tell him I'm on my way."

"I'll take care of the animals and lock up," Polly said. That meant she would let the clinic pets, Charlie the cat and Maxwell the dog, into Harriet's attached house before she left.

"Thank you." Harriet grabbed her jacket off the coatrack by the door and stepped out into the late afternoon sunlight. The garden was in full bloom, the flowers scenting the air with the sweetest perfume, and her home was beautiful, bathed in the golden light. May was her favorite month in England so far, with its longer days and gleaming sunshine. The lights were on inside the art gallery where her grandfather's paintings were displayed, and several cars were parked out front.

Harriet pulled out her phone and called Will. It rang a couple of times, and then he answered.

"Hey," Will said. His voice was rich and deep, and its warmth came through even over the phone. "How are you?"

"I'm doing well," Harriet said. "But I have a change of plans. Van called and asked me to come check out a lobster at the Whitby Marina."

"A lobster?"

"I have no idea why. But apparently the police are there."

"That sounds serious. What did the lobster do? Do you think it robbed a bank? Are they going to put it in lobster prison?" Will joked.

Harriet laughed. "I'm told it's 'in distress,' whatever that means with a lobster. But I need to head down there now, so I was wondering if you'd want to meet somewhere when I'm done, or if you want to come with me and get dinner after."

Will didn't hesitate. "Oh, I must see this distressed criminal lobster. I'll come with you."

That was exactly what she'd hoped he'd say. "Great. How about I come pick you up in a few minutes? Are you at the church or at home?"

"I just got home," Will said. "My commute was terrible today."

Harriet rolled her eyes. Will lived at the parsonage, which was next door to the church. "I'll be there in a few minutes."

"See you soon."

Harriet climbed into the old Land Rover—or "the Beast" as she called it—that she'd inherited from her grandfather along with the clinic. She drove the short distance to White Church, a beautiful old stone building overlooking the sea north of the town. It had quickly become her church home when she'd moved to White Church Bay last summer, and dating the minister only made her love the place more. She stopped in front of the parsonage, a stone cottage behind the main building.

Before she had a chance to park, Will came out.

"Hi," he said, climbing into the passenger seat. "I wasn't sure if this lobster would be dangerous, so I brought a pocketknife."

"You can never be too prepared."

Instead of setting her GPS for Whitby Marina, she'd rely on Will, since he knew the way. Whitby was about fifteen minutes north of White Church Bay, and Harriet knew roughly where the marina was, but she hadn't yet been in Yorkshire a year, and she wasn't familiar with all the back roads yet.

The country lane was quiet, shaded by mature trees lush with fresh green leaves. She'd adapted to driving on the left side of the road, but the narrow country lanes, some too small for two cars to pass without one of them going onto the verge, still made her nervous.

She'd wound her way up the hill that led out of town and was driving along a flat section edged by purple heather and bright yellow rapeseed blossoms when her phone pinged with a text.

"Could you read that to me if it's from Polly?" she asked Will.

He obliged. "'Van says to come to the harbor office when you get there.'"

Harriet had no idea where the harbor office was, but Will did.

He asked her about her day as they drove, and he told her about his day, and it only seemed like a few minutes later that she pulled up in front of a small gray building just beyond the entrance to the marina.

The marina itself was a long, narrow affair, with boats of every kind tied up at slips that jutted into the harbor. The parking lot was on one side, and the town of Whitby rose along the cliffs on both sides of the river, neat buildings with terra-cotta roofs, set one above the other. Like White Church Bay, Whitby was an old fishing village, and the town had grown up in fits and starts over the centuries, with tourism becoming its main industry.

Harriet parked the car, grabbed her vet bag, and then walked with Will to the harbor office. When she opened the door, she was surprised to see Sergeant Adam Oduba and Detective Inspector Kerry McCormick in addition to Van inside the small building. Both the sergeant and the inspector worked for the county, and they got involved when an issue was beyond the scope of the local police force.

"This must be some lobster," Will said as they walked inside.

"Hello, Dr. Bailey." Sergeant Oduba smiled at her. "Thank you for coming. Good evening, Reverend."

Harriet and Will greeted the officers, the man with gray hair and a mustache at the desk, and Van, who stood by the wall.

"I have to admit I'm quite curious," Harriet said. "I've never been called to treat a lobster before."

"DC Worthington suggested you might be the best one to help, given the odd circumstances," DI McCormick said.

"You're the one I would trust to treat any kind of animal," Van said. "Even a lobster."

"We came right away. We wanted to know what crime this lobster committed," Will said, smiling.

"*Will* wanted to know that," Harriet clarified.

"Theft," Sergeant Oduba said with a straight face. "Grand larceny, to be specific. Breaking and entering, antiquities trafficking, potentially some other charges, but we're not sure yet."

"The lobster did all that?" Harriet asked.

"No. He's just an innocent crustacean bystander," DI McCormick said. "Well, maybe an accessory after the fact. Come on. I'll show you."

More confused than ever, Harriet followed the detective inspector and Sergeant Oduba to a small room at the rear of the office, where a lobster sat in a clear plastic storage bin filled with water. She'd seen enough lobsters in that seafaring part of the country not to be surprised by the fact that it was blue. Most European lobsters were a deep navy blue color, as opposed to the American version, which was more of a muddy brown. Both species turned bright red when cooked.

"See that thing caught in its shell?" Sergeant Oduba asked.

Harriet glanced down and noticed that there was indeed a small, rust-colored object caught in a gap between two sections of the exoskeleton that made up the lobster's abdomen.

"What is that?" Harriet asked, leaning forward. Thankfully, someone had slipped rubber bands around the lobster's claws, so she wasn't worried about being pinched.

"It's a coin," DI McCormick said. "A very old and valuable one."

"We were hoping you'd be able to get it out without damaging it," Sergeant Oduba said.

"Or the lobster," DI McCormick added.

"I'll do my best," Harriet said. She rummaged in her vet bag for a pair of rubber tweezers and thick gloves. She grasped the coin with the tweezers and tugged gently. It didn't move. "It's stuck in there pretty tight, isn't it?"

She gently pressed the sections of the lobster's tail on either side of the coin. The tail flexed, and more of the coin was exposed. If she had three hands, she could use the tweezers to get it out.

"Would you mind trying with the tweezers?" she asked Will.

"This is exciting. I've never done lobster surgery before," Will said, gamely picking up the tweezers. He reached in and pulled gently on the coin. He had to tug for a minute, but then it popped out.

Sergeant Oduba immediately slipped on plastic gloves. He picked up the coin and studied it. "It matches the others," he told DI McCormick.

Others? Harriet studied the lobster for any damage to the soft parts beneath the shell. Though her eye wasn't practiced with lobsters, this one didn't seem to have any wounds. She set the lobster back into the container and straightened up. "What is the coin? What's so important about it?"

DI McCormick spoke. "It's a Norse coin, probably from the ancient Viking settlements near here."

"There were Vikings in England?"

"Yes. A Norse settlement outside of York dates to the early Middle Ages," DI McCormick explained.

"Oh my." Harriet studied the rusty metal. Suddenly, she understood why she'd been called out for a lobster. It wasn't the lobster they cared about—it was the coin. That made much more sense. "If it's that old, it should be in a museum."

"Funny you should mention that," DI McCormick said. "This is part of a collection that was stolen from a local museum last month."

"And it was found this afternoon inside a lobster trap at the bottom of the North Sea," Van said. "Along with other old stuff."

"As in, this is considerably bigger than a single coin stuck in a lobster's shell?" Harriet asked.

Sergeant Oduba sighed. "This is still an active investigation. We can't—"

"She has a right to know at least this much, given that she did surgery on a lobster for us," DI McCormick told him.

Harriet hadn't actually done any surgery, but her curiosity convinced her not to point that out. DI McCormick wasn't usually so forthcoming, so Harriet didn't want to press her luck.

"A man was out on the water this afternoon checking his father's lobster traps, but he got a little turned around," the inspector went on. "He accidentally pulled one up that wasn't his, and he found more than lobsters. He found several sealed rubber containers inside the trap. He thought that was odd, especially since one of the containers popped open and a few old coins spilled out."

"The lobster was inside the trap, along with the containers?" Will asked.

DI McCormick nodded. "He looked inside the container and saw that it held dozens of coins, which he quickly recognized as being very old."

"Good thing he did. I wouldn't have thought they were anything important," Van said.

Harriet didn't want to say it out loud, but she was pretty sure she wouldn't have realized they were important either if she'd come across them. The one she'd seen simply resembled a piece of rusted metal.

"He's a history teacher at the local high school, apparently," Sergeant Oduba said. "He couldn't tell exactly what they were, but he knew enough to figure they didn't belong in a lobster trap at the bottom of the sea."

"You said there were other containers," Will said. "Did he open those to see what was in them?"

"He did. He managed to pry open the other two, and that was when he knew he needed to report it," DI McCormick said. "He radioed the local police."

"We keep a couple police boats in the harbor, so I took one out to meet him and take possession of the trap," Van said.

"What was in the other containers?" Harriet asked.

"An old bust and a bowl," Van said. He pointed to a table nearby, where two more plastic containers sat open. From where she stood

Harriet could see that one held a small bust and the other a bowl made from some kind of clay. "Really old."

"We're still waiting on analysis, but the man who found them thought the bust might be from Roman times. The bowl he wasn't sure about."

Roman times. Harriet had heard something about that. The Romans occupied England centuries before, and the country still bore remnants of their ancient influence.

"Were those objects stolen from museums too?" Harriet asked.

"We don't know yet," DI McCormick said. "But we're investigating."

Harriet struggled to wrap her mind around what she was hearing. "Viking coins and Roman busts in a lobster trap in the North Sea? How did they get there?"

For a moment, no one spoke. Then DI McCormick let out a breath. "We don't know. But our best guess at this point is that someone was using the trap as a holding station or a dead drop, a place to stash the stolen items where they were very unlikely to be found until someone could pick them up."

"And when they were picked up? What then?" Harriet asked.

"We assume they would have been taken by boat to an international port somewhere," Sergeant Oduba finally said. "But we don't know for sure."

"You mean someone was trying to smuggle these antiquities out of the country," Harriet said.

The police officers all nodded, and Harriet understood that this thing—whatever it was—went way beyond lobsters.

CHAPTER TWO

alf an hour later, Will and Harriet walked toward an outdoor table at the Cliffside Chippy, a casual takeout place in White Church Bay that was famous for its fish and chips, which Harriet had always known as french fries. Golden sunlight bathed the area around the picnic tables in a warm glow. Below them, the sound of the waves pounding against the rocks announced that it was high tide. Will led them to a table and set their food down, and then he tapped his pocket before he sat on the bench.

"I understood about half of what happened back there," Harriet said, sprinkling salt and vinegar over her meal. She'd learned that custom during her time in Yorkshire, and every so often the combination was exactly what she craved. "What about you?"

Although he'd grown up on the moors, Will's family was from Muckle Roe, one of the Shetland islands off the coast of Scotland, and he'd spent plenty of time on boats. "I followed it well enough," he said. "What do you have questions about?"

"First, tell me about lobster traps and how they work."

Will sipped his ginger ale then pulled out his phone and typed something. He showed her the screen. "Well, this is what they look like."

It was a wire cage, about the size of a bale of hay. In the photo, there were several cages, painted yellow and blue as well as plain metal, piled in large stacks. She'd often seen such items used as decor in seafood restaurants.

"So, lobster season is in the summer," Will said. "Late May or June through September."

"Is that because lobster bakes are more fun when it's warm out?"

"Definitely. There's also something about the currents and water temperature and other trivial things." Will grinned. "But mostly it's about lobster bakes."

"Good to know. How does the trap work?"

"You take your trap with the bait inside and drop it down to the sea floor. When a lobster comes along and smells the bait, it goes in through here." Will pointed to a round hole on the end of a trap. "But because the trap narrows, once the lobster is in, it can't get back out. It hangs out in there, eating tiny shrimp and whatever else floats by, until the fisherman comes along and pulls the trap up. He checks to make sure the lobster is big enough for him to harvest. If so, he can either take it home or sell it to a restaurant or something, depending on his licensing. If he can't collect it, he releases it."

"Once the fishermen put the traps in the water, how do they find them again?" She cut into her fried fish, and steam wafted up in curly white wisps.

"That's what the buoys attached to the traps are for."

"You mean they're not just cool coastal decorations?" Harriet quipped. Many of the buildings in town had collections of buoys hung on the outside. Nothing said idyllic seaside village like walls of buoys.

Will laughed. "They're good for that as well." He ate a few fries before he continued. "Each lobster collector has his own distinctive buoy colors and pattern so they can tell whose are whose."

"So, when DI McCormick said someone pulled up the wrong trap, it's because the colors and the pattern on the buoy were close enough to his to cause confusion."

"Exactly. And unfortunately for whoever's trap was full of valuable antiques, it shouldn't be too hard for the police to track the owner. You have to register your color scheme with your permit."

"So it should be an easy case to solve," Harriet said.

"I would think so," Will said. "I don't have a boat myself, but Kyle Manning from church lets me borrow his sometimes. I could take you out to show you different buoys, if you'd like." Kyle was in his midforties, owned a woolens shop in town, and sang in the church choir. "He doesn't get to use it as much as he likes, and I guess he's pretty sure I'm not going to steal it, being his minister and all."

"And he isn't afraid you don't know how to drive it?"

Will shook his head. "I grew up on boats. I was in the junior coast guard during my high school years. I'm not saying I'd never make a mistake out on the water, but he trusts me enough to let me use it sometimes."

"Then let's do it. It sounds fun."

He smiled at her over his fried fish. "I'll set it up with Kyle."

Harriet took a bite of the flaky fish, savoring how the vinegar she'd added brought a bright note to the taste. "So now can you explain to me why someone would try to smuggle historical artifacts out of the country in a lobster trap?"

"It's actually kind of genius," Will said. "I mean, of course it's wrong, but it's genius too. Lobster traps are pretty much left alone in the bay. The person who checks them is usually the person who dropped them, so it wouldn't be hard to take the artifacts out on a boat, seal them in a waterproof container, stash them in a lobster trap, and then leave them there until you're ready to pick them up."

"Except in this case, the plot was discovered because someone got confused and pulled up the wrong trap."

"Sure, but this is the first time I've ever heard of that happening," Will said. "People know their buoys. The officers said the teacher was checking traps for his father, which could explain how he got confused. If the person who stole the artifacts wanted to hide them, this was a good idea, especially if they were trying to smuggle them out of the country. That would almost have to be the plan, since the items themselves are much more likely to be recognized here in England. So what's the best way to do that?"

Harriet thought for a moment. "When you fly, the airlines scan your luggage. They know what's inside before they let you on a plane." When she'd flown into Heathrow to move to England, she didn't have to answer any customs questions or fill out any forms about what was in her luggage, because it had already been scanned. "So if you were trying to smuggle stolen goods out that way, they might catch it."

"They often don't scan luggage on trains," Will said. "Perhaps you could take a train—except that England is an island."

"There's the Chunnel to France," Harriet said, referring to the train that ran underneath the English Channel.

"True, but they scan your luggage before you get on that train, since it goes internationally. Even a boat is tricky, because the coast guard inspects vessels entering and leaving major ports."

"I wouldn't think Whitby would qualify as a major port," Harriet said.

Will grinned at her. "Probably not. And the marina is shallow enough that you can only really take a boat of any meaningful size in or out at high tide. At low tide, it's so shallow that anything but small boats would get stuck. In either case, you'd want a very big boat if you were aiming for Amsterdam, which is the closest big port." He took a bite of his fish and swallowed before saying, "Although, I guess technically you could probably take a smaller boat south along the coast and then leave from Dover or Margate to cross the Channel. From there you could get to Ostend easily enough."

"Ostend is where?"

"Belgium. Not far from Bruges."

Harriet nodded, though she wasn't totally sure where that was. Her grasp of European geography wasn't as great as she would have liked.

"But if you did that, you'd be sailing along English waters, which is a risk if you were carrying stolen artifacts with you," Will continued. "Better to leave them in international waters for someone in a bigger boat to pick up and take to Amsterdam for you. It's actually pretty smart. If you use a small boat to get your goods out into the open water and don't leave from a major port, you're halfway there."

"But who left the artifacts in the lobster trap?" Harriet mused. "Was it the same person who stole them in the first place?"

"I guess that's what the police will try to find out," Will said.

Harriet supposed he was right. As curious as she was, the police were on it, and she should leave it to them.

"Thank you for coming with me," she said.

"Of course. It's the most exciting thing that's happened to me in weeks. It's not every day you meet a lobster that's been accused of breaking and entering, grand larceny, and possession of stolen goods." Will chuckled.

She loved that he made her laugh. She loved that she could count on him. She loved—well, him. Sometimes she couldn't believe how much God had blessed her.

As they finished their meals, the conversation moved on to other topics. Will talked about a new-membership class he was leading at the church later that week, and Harriet told him about a llama she'd treated for a bacterial infection earlier in the day.

"Oh, my dad called. He's been cleaning out my late grandmother's attic and found some sentimental heirlooms, and he wanted to let me know he was sending me a few things."

"That's nice," Harriet said. "Like what?"

There was a beat before he answered, "Some old books she loved, mostly."

"How wonderful. What books?"

He took a sip of his soda before he continued. "Um...I think one of them was *Ivanhoe*?"

It wasn't a strange thing to say. But the way he said it made her feel like there was something he was leaving unsaid.

But she wasn't going to pry. "That's one of those classics I feel like I should have read but never have."

"She loved Sir Walter Scott. He's basically a national hero in Scotland."

"I didn't know that." Will seemed to be distracted, and she was almost glad when his phone rang. He apologized and pulled it out of his pocket. "It's Myles Stafford."

Myles was an eightysomething-year-old member of White Church. Harriet knew Will paid special attention to calls from the elderly members. If someone was in the hospital or needed help, he wanted to know right away.

"Go ahead and answer it," she said.

He smiled and put the phone to his ear. Harriet couldn't hear Myles's end of the conversation, but she saw Will's face change as he listened to whatever Myles had to say. Then Will said, "I'm with Harriet Bailey at the moment. Do you mind if I bring her with me?" After what must have been agreement, he said, "We'll be right there."

Will hung up and said, "The police just showed up at Myles's house. Apparently, they think he stole those artifacts."

"What?" Harriet shook her head. Myles was a soft-spoken retired commercial fisherman. He had a blind rescue dog and played board games every week with other elderly members at the church. "He couldn't have. How could they even think Myles might have done something like that?"

"I have no idea. But he asked me to come over and tell the police that myself."

"Then let's go."

CHAPTER THREE

Myles lived in a stone cottage draped with ivy and climbing roses. Harriet had never been there before, but it wasn't hard to find, because of the police car in front. She parked and followed Will up the cobblestone path toward the door. Through the wooden fence, she saw half a dozen buoys tacked to the side of the house, decorating a small sitting area in the backyard.

Will knocked on the door, and Myles opened it, his thin white hair askew and his eyes wide. "Thank you for coming, Pastor," he said. "Good to see you, Harriet."

"Of course," Will said, and Harriet gave him a smile that she hoped was encouraging.

They followed him into the living room, where Sergeant Oduba, DI McCormick, and Van sat on stiff-backed chairs before a roaring fire. Judging by the low ceilings and the cramped room, the cottage was very old. "It's good to see you again," Will said, nodding at the police officers. "Though I had no idea it would be so soon."

"Pastor, can you please tell them I didn't steal anything?" Myles said. "I didn't even collect lobsters this year."

Will looked at the detective inspector. "Perhaps you could tell us what's going on?"

"Of course," she said. "The lobster trap with the artifacts was attached to a buoy painted in a particular pattern with navy blue and orange stripes. We checked with the Department of Marine Fisheries, and that color combination and pattern is registered to Myles Stafford."

"But I didn't register any traps this year," Myles said. "It's too hard for me to haul the traps by myself, so I can only check them when my son is around. He moved to Scotland a few months ago, and he doesn't make it home very often. Whoever registered those traps, it wasn't me." He folded his arms over his chest. "I didn't steal any historical artifacts. And even if I did, why would I put them in a lobster trap at the bottom of the sea?"

"Is it possible someone else registered the trap in Myles's name?" Will asked the police officers.

"If someone applied for that permit using false information, we will of course need to track them down," DI McCormick said.

"Do you know anyone who could have taken out a permit in your name?" Harriet asked Myles. She ducked her head when the three officers looked at her. "Sorry. Your investigation."

The corner of the inspector's mouth quirked up. "It is, but we do need the answer to that question, Mr. Stafford."

Myles shook his head. "I can't think of who would do such a thing."

"All right. Well, thank you for your time," DI McCormick said, standing. "We appreciate you talking with us. Please don't leave town."

"I'm not going anywhere. You know I didn't do it, right?" Myles said. "Pastor, can you tell them I didn't do it?"

"As Myles's pastor, I can attest that it would be highly out of character for him to have taken part in any kind of theft," Will said.

That seemed to settle Myles's nerves.

"Thank you, Will." Van also stood.

"We'll make a note," Sergeant Oduba said. He didn't give much away, but Harriet thought she could see amusement in his eyes. "You know, most people call a lawyer when the police show up," he added. "Not the pastor."

"Yes, well. White Church Bay is a special kind of place," Myles said. "And Pastor Will is a special kind of minister."

"We'll let you know if we have other questions," Van said as the three officers left.

Myles offered Harriet and Will a smile. "Thank you for coming."

"Of course. Happy to help. If we did, anyway," Will said. "I think you made a good case. They have to investigate, but they'll figure out who really did it."

"I sure hope so. I can't afford legal fees. If they try to charge me with it, I don't know what I'll do."

"I wouldn't worry too much about that just yet," Will said. "I'm sure they'll find whoever registered that trap in your name."

"But what if they don't?" Myles fretted. "Sometimes they need someone to pin it on to close the case."

"DI McCormick, Sergeant Oduba, and Van are all good people *and* good police officers," Will said. "They do their jobs well."

"I hope so." Myles suddenly looked at Harriet, his eyes wide. "You solve mysteries."

Harriet blinked. "Um, not in any official capacity."

"Maybe not, but you're good at it. I've heard that about you. You've figured things out that the police haven't."

"She's the best," Will said. "Harriet is brilliant at solving mysteries."

"Well, I have been able to uncover an answer or two," Harriet admitted. "But the police—"

"Can you try to figure out what happened?" Myles asked. "If you find the truth, they won't blame me for it."

Could she? Contrary to what seemed to be popular opinion, she didn't want to interfere with an official investigation. "The police are looking into it."

"And they think I did it. What motivation do they have to look elsewhere when they have an easy answer right in front of them?"

Harriet knew she should explain why she couldn't interfere, that this was a case involving grand larceny and international smuggling and she had no right to be getting in the middle of it, that she possessed none of the tools the police did.

But when she saw the genuine fear in the elderly man's eyes, she knew she couldn't simply walk away.

"I'll see what I can do," she said at last. "I doubt I'll be able to find much that the police can't, and I'm limited as to what I can do, but if it will ease your mind, I'll see if I can clear your name."

"Thank you," Myles said. "Thank you, Harriet."

Harriet had no clue where she should even start, but there was no turning back now.

The sky was already light by the time Harriet's alarm went off Tuesday morning. The longer days of May were so much nicer than the dark days of winter in that way, but it was still hard to get out of her warm, comfortable bed so early.

She rolled over and grabbed for her phone to silence the alarm. Then she pushed herself up and squinted at the screen. A text had come in overnight from Dustin Stewart. The man who'd broken off their engagement when they'd worked in the same veterinary clinic back in the States.

Her stomach dropped. She hadn't heard from him in more than a year. What did he want?

HI HARRIET, I WANTED TO LET YOU KNOW THAT I'M COMING TO ENGLAND LATER THIS WEEK. I FLY INTO LONDON ON FRIDAY, AND I WAS HOPING YOU WOULDN'T MIND IF I TOOK THE TRAIN UP TO YORKSHIRE TO SEE YOU. I'D LOVE TO TALK WITH YOU. CAN I TAKE YOU OUT FOR COFFEE? OR WOULD IT BE TEA NOW THAT YOU'RE A BONA FIDE BRIT? LET ME KNOW WHAT DAY IS GOOD FOR YOU.

Dustin wanted to meet with her? She couldn't imagine him walking around White Church Bay. It didn't fit. He was a part of her old life. He was the main thing she'd wanted to leave behind when she moved to start her new life. Perhaps it was irrational, but Harriet felt that if he came here, her new life would be tainted somehow. Better to leave the past in the past, instead of letting it infect the new goodness she'd found.

She stared at her phone, trying to figure out how to respond. She started to type a message back a few times, trying to find a way to say he shouldn't come, but after several tries, she decided she needed coffee for her nerves. She set the phone down and got out of bed. She was due at the Hamilton farm in just under an hour to administer shots to a new crop of lambs, so she needed to get going. Dustin would have to wait.

Harriet started the coffee brewing and got Maxwell, the partially paralyzed dachshund she'd inherited from her grandfather, hooked up to his wheeled prosthesis. Then she let him out into the yard, fed him and Charlie, and sat down at the table with a steaming cup of coffee and her Bible. The text from Dustin had unsettled her, and she needed to spend some time in the Word.

Harriet was slowly reading through the book of Acts, and she enjoyed learning more about the early church. Today's passage was about how Paul, a persecutor of the first Christians, was blinded on the road to Damascus and how, after three days, the scales fell from his eyes and he started to follow the Lord. He not only spent the rest of his life traveling the world to spread the message of Jesus Christ, but also wrote a fair chunk of the New Testament. It was an incredible transformation. Paul had taken full advantage of the second chance he'd been given, and its implications were still being felt in modern times.

Spiritually fortified, she ate a quick breakfast of toast and eggs. She tugged on a wool sweater, as it was a brisk May morning. Then she let Maxwell and Charlie into the clinic, where Polly would care for them once she arrived, and climbed into the Beast.

She pulled out onto the rural road and was soon passing open fields dotted with sheep, clumps of gnarled old trees, and stone outcroppings. The road rose and fell gently over the rolling hills, and around every bend were sweeping views of the moors. Harriet was beginning to suspect she would never tire of the stunning views.

She had been to the Hamilton farm before, nestled in a little hollow on the back side of a craggy hill, surrounded in all directions by the rolling moors. The farm itself was comprised of a neat stone farmhouse and several wooden barns and outbuildings. Harriet chatted with Leslie Hamilton as she inspected the lambs and gave them their shots. Leslie used her sheep's wool to create the most beautiful yarn, which she carded, spun, and dyed herself. Harriet had attended a meeting of the knitting group at church a few months before, and it had given her a deeper appreciation for high-quality yarn.

When she was done at the farm, Harriet climbed into her vehicle to head back to the clinic, but she realized she had some time before she needed to be there for her first in-clinic appointment of the day. She was halfway to Whitby anyway. Maybe she should swing by the marina and see if she could talk to anyone who might be able to tell her more about the person who registered for the lobster permit in Myles's name.

She made the short drive to the marina and found the harbor office. When she tried the door, it was locked, which reminded her that not everyone started their workday when farms did. There was another building on the other side of the parking lot, and the lights were on inside. The sign above the door read MARINA OFFICE. She decided to poke her head in and see if anyone could help her.

The office consisted of a small waiting area and a counter with two desks behind it. Overhead fluorescent lights buzzed and flickered in the quiet room, which had gray carpet. Aerial shots of the marina and boating safety posters dotted the otherwise beige walls.

"Can I help you?" A fortysomething woman with brown hair caught up in a clip smiled at Harriet from behind one of the desks. There were tidy stacks of paper covering her desk, as well as a name plate that said MARTINA PADAVANO.

Now that she was there, Harriet wasn't exactly sure what she even wanted to ask. Finally, she settled on, "I was wondering how I might find out about registering to put down lobster traps."

"Are you wanting to harvest lobsters yourself?" Martina asked.

"No," Harriet said. "Generally, I'd like to know more about the process of getting a license. Specifically, I'm interested in finding out about someone in particular who's taken out a license to harvest lobsters."

Martina's gaze sharpened. "I see. There's been a lot of interest in that particular topic lately."

Harriet assumed she meant the police, but she wasn't sure how to respond. Did Martina know about the discovery yesterday?

Fortunately, Martina continued without needing a response. "I can tell you what the process entails, but unless you're with the police, I can't give you any specific information about existing permit registrations."

"I'm not with the police," Harriet said. "But I would like to understand the process."

"Right," Martina said. "The short answer is that if you want to collect lobsters, you fill out a form. We only issue a certain number of permits per year, so you have to act quickly. Then we file your application with the relevant authorities. After that, you pay a small fee, tell us what color scheme your buoys will have, and you're golden. Each permit allows you to set a specific number of traps."

"And you can put the traps anywhere?" Harriet asked.

"Anywhere your heart desires. Some people claim they know the best spots, but they don't seem to have any more luck than anyone else, if you ask me. Lobsters go where they want to. Trying to outsmart them is a fool's game."

"Do you require proof of identification when someone files for a permit?"

"We don't. People simply drop off the form and their fee, and that's it." She cocked her head. "Why are you asking these questions?"

Harriet decided it was best to share what she knew. "The police came here yesterday and asked about a lobster trap marked with an orange and navy blue buoy, right?"

"That's right," Martina said hesitantly.

"The trap was registered to Myles Stafford. But I spoke with Myles last night, and he insists he didn't file a request for a permit this year. He thinks someone registered for the license in his name."

Martina's eyes widened. "Really?"

"Do you remember anything about the person who registered for the permit under that name?"

"I don't," Martina said, shaking her head. "I'm sorry. We register dozens of permits, both commercial and recreational, and I haven't been at this job all that long. I don't know everyone, or even most of the people yet."

"So Myles Stafford is not a name you know?"

"Not off the top of my head."

"He used to be a commercial fisherman out of this marina, and then he collected lobsters for himself for many years after that. He's in his eighties, if that helps," Harriet said.

"I would have remembered him in that case. We don't get many people that age filing for lobster permits. You have to be strong to hoist the trap up. Even if you use a winch to raise it, you still have to have the strength to toss it back in the water, and that's not easy. If this guy is in his eighties, he definitely wasn't the person who came in to register."

"I don't suppose you could tell me anything about who did file," Harriet said. "I don't want to compromise your ethics or anything, but if we can learn any details, that would be helpful."

"Usually, I wouldn't dream of it, for privacy reasons. However, since it wasn't actually Myles, I don't suppose we're violating his privacy." Martina selected a manila folder, thumbed through the papers inside, and pulled one out. "It appears the person filed for the permit as soon as registration opened. This is my signature, so I took the form, but I didn't note anything strange about it." She tapped the page. "Whoever the guy was, he listed his birthday as July 15, 1986. I think I would have flagged it if he was in his eighties. I'm bad with ages, but I'm not that bad."

"If he was telling the truth, that means he's in his late thirties," Harriet said. "That's something to go on."

"It's not much though," Martina said with obvious regret. "I think it's very likely it was a man, at least. I would have noticed if a woman applied with the name Myles."

"Here's what I don't get," Harriet said. "Why use someone else's name at all? Why not simply make up a fake name?"

"Unfortunately, we don't have enough permits for everyone who wants one. We're trying to prevent overharvesting of the lobster population. People who are renewing permits or have gotten permits in the past get to file a few days before it opens to the general public. Maybe whoever filed knew the real Myles wasn't planning to renew his permit this year."

"So he was able to take Myles's spot," Harriet filled in. "I hate to say it, but that's pretty smart. He even thought to put in his own birth date—or at least one that was feasible given his appearance—so as not to set off any red flags. Whoever processed the application must not have noticed the discrepancy between Myles's birthdate last year versus this year."

Martina sighed. "Oh dear. This is a real mess, isn't it?"

"It's starting to appear that way. Do you have any ideas about who it could have been?" Harriet asked.

Martina shook her head. "One name comes to mind as someone who would know how to manipulate the system that well, but this couldn't have been O'Grady. He's too well-known around here. He would never get away with something like this without being recognized."

"O'Grady?"

"A fisherman named Shane O'Grady. He has a bit of a reputation for underhanded dealings. But like I said, it wasn't him. I'm positive."

"But if you don't ask for ID, anyone could have posed as Myles when applying," Harriet said. "This O'Grady could have paid someone to come in and submit the application for him, right?"

"I suppose so." Martina's shoulders slumped in defeat. "I may need to suggest some changes to our system going forward. Starting with proof of identification. For now, I'm afraid I can't think of anything more. I wish I knew who it was, but I don't."

"If I wanted to talk to Shane O'Grady, do you know how I could reach him?" Harriet asked.

"Down at the pub in White Church Bay would be your best bet. The Crow's Nest. He's there most nights, from what I understand."

Harriet thanked Martina and gave her a business card, asking her to call if she thought of anything else. Then she headed to the clinic. The first patients of the day would arrive shortly, and she did have her actual job to do.

CHAPTER FOUR

Polly smiled a greeting from her desk when Harriet walked inside the clinic, and a black poodle mix jumped up to meet her. The owner, a man Harriet was sure she'd seen before but whose name she couldn't recall, pulled on the leash to keep the dog from launching itself at her.

"Good morning," Polly called. "How were the lambs?"

"Adorable, of course." Harriet closed the door behind her and stepped forward to pet the poodle mix. "Well, hello," she said to the dog, who immediately jumped up again, his front legs reaching for her. "You're very friendly, aren't you?"

"Sit, Sirius," the man said, but the dog was too interested in making a new friend. He continued to flail his front legs to try to reach her.

With that, the morning began in earnest. She examined Sirius and wrote out a prescription for a medication that would help with his digestive tract issue, and then she saw a cat named Philip for a wellness visit. The rest of the morning flew by in a rush of pets, one after another, and she didn't stand still until Polly called a break for lunch.

Harriet returned from the hasty sandwich in her kitchen to an empty waiting room.

"Do we have a longer break than I thought?" she asked Polly. Charlie was perched on the edge of the counter. Harriet scratched the cat's head absently, and Charlie began to purr. Grandad had named all his clinic cats Charlie, regardless of gender, to make it easier for him to remember.

"Winnie the Yorkie is running a bit late, but she'll be here soon," Polly said.

"Well, I'll take the break," Harriet said.

"If you want, you can use it to return a message. Ida called from the gallery. Something about an intern who wants to talk to you," Polly said.

Harriet nodded. "I'll go over there after we're done today."

"That sounds good," Polly said. Then she leaned forward on her elbows. "I heard there was quite the to-do about that lobster last night."

"Indeed. Apparently, the lobster was in possession of stolen antiquities."

"I've always said you can't trust a lobster," Polly joked.

Harriet laughed. "The thing is, the trap that caught the thieving lobster was registered under a false name, so it's not as straight-forward as it would appear to find out who's behind it. Or, rather, it was falsely registered under someone else's name."

"Really?"

Harriet filled Polly in on what had happened at Myles's home, and her trip to the marina earlier that morning.

"So they don't know who actually registered that trap?" Polly asked.

"No, though a name was floated. Have you ever heard of Shane O'Grady?"

"You mean *Shady* O'Grady? Oh yeah. He's quite the character."

"Shady?" Harriet wanted to laugh, despite herself.

"Everyone calls him that. Not to his face, of course. He's got quite the reputation. I don't remember all the details, but there was something in the paper about stealing mussels. I bet you could look it up. And then there was the time he disabled a refrigerator in a fish market one night."

"Yikes," Harriet said. "That couldn't have been pleasant to walk into the next day. Why would he do that?"

"I don't know. I just remember reading that all the fish spoiled. Security camera footage showed Shane doing it, so they caught him right away."

"If he was caught on camera, he must not be a particularly savvy criminal."

"You'd have to check the details. I'm not sure I'm remembering everything totally right. But yeah, that's why he's Shady O'Grady. And if you're thinking he might be behind the lobster thing—well, I wouldn't be surprised. He has a boat and knows about lobster traps. Plus, that's just the kind of thing he might do. I doubt he knows a lot about antiquities, but who's to say?"

"Maybe he didn't do the actual theft," Harriet said. "He might simply be a delivery guy of some kind."

"You're right," Polly said. "I'd say he's a likely suspect."

In that case, Harriet was sure the police were already looking into him. But that didn't mean she couldn't do some more digging.

Winnie the Yorkie arrived with her owner, and Harriet spent the next few hours tending to animals. She hadn't forgotten the text from Dustin, but there wasn't really time to think about it in the midst of treating patients.

Once their last client left, it didn't take long to clean and close the office. Polly headed home, and Harriet walked across the parking area to the small art gallery on the property. She thought it might be the prettiest building in White Church Bay, with its thatched roof and windows of wavy glass. Roses and wisteria climbed up the side of the building, in full bloom.

Harriet opened the door and walked inside. The white walls were covered with Grandad's paintings—animal scenes, a few still lifes, and a number of landscapes of the windswept English countryside.

"Hello, Harriet," said Ida. Her strawberry-blond hair was pulled back in a short ponytail, and she wore a blazer over a light-colored blouse. Ida Winslow managed the gallery, which maintained Grandad's legacy as a beloved artist.

"Hi, Ida. Polly mentioned that you called."

"I did. I wanted to introduce you to Riley Sloane." She turned toward a young woman sitting at the computer at the rear of the gallery.

Riley stood and came to greet Harriet. She was dressed simply in fitted slacks and a gray sweater, and her long brown hair framed her face. She wore thick-framed glasses and a thin gold necklace, and she smiled widely as she approached.

"Riley is studying art over at the university in Whitby. She heard something about you seeing some antiques," Ida said.

"It's so wonderful to meet you," Riley said brightly. "I've been a fan of your grandfather's work for so long, and it's an honor to be able to intern here."

"I'm glad to meet you too. I'm sure Ida is happy to have you," Harriet said.

"I have some things to take care of, so I'll leave you two to chat." Ida hurried away, leaving them in the large open room.

"Thank you for coming over to talk to me," Riley said. "Like I said, I'm thrilled to meet you, but when I heard that you actually saw the antiquities that they pulled out of the water, I knew I had to try to see you. I'm studying ancient art, and I wrote a paper about one of the pieces that was found yesterday."

"Really?" That was an amazing coincidence, but Harriet had another, more urgent thought. "How do you know anything was found?" As far as she knew, the news about their recovery hadn't been made public.

"Oh, Professor Russell—he's my advisor—told me. He was the one the police called on to tell them what the things were because he's a leading expert on ancient art and archaeology. He consults on museum collections and leads digs and things like that. He got to see what they found, which is so awesome. He said it was incredible—all those amazing pieces, just sitting at the bottom of the sea."

"It was pretty incredible," Harriet admitted, wondering if the police knew that the professor was sharing information with his students.

"But he also mentioned that one of the coins from the Norse period was stuck in the shell of a lobster, and that the police were going to call a vet from White Church Bay to get it out without hurting the coin."

"How did you know it was me?" Harriet asked. "I'm not the only vet in White Church Bay."

"Dr. Russell specified that it was a female vet, so it wasn't hard to narrow it down."

Harriet sighed. Perhaps someday, a woman being a veterinarian wouldn't be quite so unique.

"Since you saw the artifacts too, I wondered if I could ask you about them."

"The coin lodged in the lobster shell was the only piece I saw up close," Harriet said. "I did catch a glimpse of the bust and the bowl, but I didn't have a chance to study them. Not that I would have understood what I was seeing."

"They are fascinating artifacts representing thousands of years of British history. Dr. Russell said the bowl was from the people who lived in Yorkshire during the Stone Age, thousands of years ago. It's a physical connection between branches of humanity that would otherwise never interact. And the bust they found—the one I wrote my paper about last semester—is of Marcus Aurelius, from when the Romans occupied Britain."

Harriet's head began to spin. "Right. When exactly was that?"

"They first took over around 43 AD. The Romans occupied Britain for about 400 years."

"Whoa. That's a few years after Jesus was crucified."

"Exactly. It was the early days of the Church, right around when Paul started his missionary journeys. We're talking Roman Forum, feed-the-Christians-to-the-lions-in-the-Coliseum era."

Harriet had never really thought about how the timeline of the Bible matched up with—and influenced—things she'd read about in history class once upon a time. "That's amazing."

Riley bounced on her toes. "Isn't it? And this bust of Marcus Aurelius must have been brought over from Rome during his rule as emperor, which was only about a hundred years after that. Dr. Russell said the piece was in near-pristine condition, and because it's an image of the emperor, it's one of the most important objects in England from that time period."

Suddenly Harriet wished she'd paid more attention to the bust when she'd seen it yesterday. "So someone stole it from a museum?"

"No, believe it or not. The Norse coins were stolen from a museum, but the bust was held in a private collection."

"Something that old and important wasn't in a museum?"

Riley pressed her lips together in clear disapproval and then said, "Sadly, many of the most priceless items aren't. There was a time when owning ancient artifacts was very much in vogue among the upper class, so even now a lot of our cultural heritage is locked away in private homes throughout the country. This bust was held here in Yorkshire. That's why I chose it for my paper. I hoped I might be able to actually examine it myself, but I wasn't able to get access to it in the end."

"The owner wouldn't let you see it to write a paper about it?"

"I couldn't even get the owner—some baron—to return my emails about it. I called a couple times, and the housekeeper told me she'd pass along the message, but he never called me back. I guess he's kind of a recluse or something." Riley seemed to shake off her annoyance. "It's okay though. I read a newspaper article about the piece from when his grandfather acquired it, so at least I saw a picture of it. I was able to find enough about it from other sources, but it sure would have been better if I'd been able to see the real thing. I should have just written my paper about the Elgin Marbles like everybody else." She grinned. "It would have been a lot simpler."

Harriet had seen the Elgin Marbles—a sculpture collection taken from the interior of the Parthenon in ancient Greece and plundered by the adventuring "preservationist" Earl of Elgin in the nineteenth century—in the British Museum years ago.

But something about Riley's description caught Harriet's attention. Lord in a fancy house, Yorkshire, recluse...this was starting to sound like someone she knew.

"Can I ask who the owner of the bust was?"

"Lord Liam Beresford," Riley said.

"I know him."

"What?" Riley's eyes widened. "How on earth do you know him?"

"It's a long story." Harriet didn't want to recount the full tale of how she'd tried to return the baron's wandering dog, only to find him missing with no one aware of his whereabouts. "He doesn't do email, to my knowledge. And he really does keep to himself. It's nothing personal. Mrs. Lewis wasn't lying when she called him a recluse."

"You know the housekeeper too?"

"A little. I'm just saying I'm not surprised you didn't hear back from him," Harriet said. "He's a nice man, but very private." It was a shame he wouldn't help a university student though. He didn't like visitors, but his refusal to help felt out of character for him. She wondered what had happened. "I would love to read your paper, if you're willing."

Riley's face lit up. "Really?"

"Really. I'd like to learn more about the bust."

"I'd be happy to email it to you." She took out her phone. "What's your address?"

Harriet gave it to her and then asked, "Do you know anything about the bowl or coins that were also found in the trap?"

"Not much," Riley said. "I think that stuff is cool and all, but I'm more interested in ancient Greece and Rome, personally. The bowl and the coins are useful, everyday objects, so they're more archaeology or history. I prefer art for art's sake, like the bust."

It was an interesting distinction, and one Harriet hadn't thought of. She supposed Riley was right.

Riley glanced out the window. "My ride is here. I better get going."

"Thank you for talking to me about this."

"No, thank *you*. Not everyone is interested in letting me babble on like that." Riley grabbed her bag and hurried out the door.

CHAPTER FIVE

arriet's phone rang as she crossed the parking lot toward the clinic. For a moment, she held her breath. What if it was Dustin? Should she answer it? She glanced down at the screen.

And breathed a sigh of relief. It was Will. She answered at once. "Hi."

"Are you free this evening?" he asked.

"For my favorite handsome guy? Always."

"I hope that's me," Will joked.

"Of course it is."

"Glad to hear it. Anyway, I asked Kyle about his boat, and he said I could use it tomorrow, or he offered to take us out while he checks his lobster traps tonight. Are you interested in going tonight?"

"You bet." Perhaps she'd glean some tidbit that would help connect the dots as to who might have tried to frame Myles.

"He says it'll be high tide in a couple of hours. He can meet us there at six thirty. How about I pick you up a little after six?"

"That sounds great."

"See you then."

Harriet had some time before Will would pick her up, so she checked her email and saw that Riley had sent her the academic paper she'd written about the bust.

Art History 203: The Art of the Classical World
THE HEAD OF THE EMPEROR: WHAT AN ANCIENT
PIECE OF NATIONAL PROPAGANDA
CAN TELL US ABOUT LIFE IN ROMAN BRITAIN
By Riley Sloane

As far as empires go, the colonial reach of the British is matched only by the ancient Romans, who conquered most of the known world in the early centuries of the Common Era. When soldiers were sent from Rome to subdue the wilds of what we now know as England, their goal was utter domination. But in the years that followed, when settlers from Rome moved to the region to build cities and spread the Roman way of life, they brought many important cultural objects with them. One such object was a bust of Emperor Marcus Aurelius, the crown jewel of a cache of Roman artifacts discovered in a Yorkshire dig in 1948.

Marcus Aurelius reigned as the last of the "five good emperors" of Rome (the others being Nerva, Trajan, Hadrian, and Antonius Pius), holding the throne from 161-180 CE. After Aurelius's death, the empire fell into civil war and broke apart. During his reign, Aurelius was lauded as a fair leader, and his idealized image was distributed widely throughout the Roman world. This common practice served as a tangible reminder to all Roman citizens of whom they served and was also used as an object of devotion.

The Imperial Cult—or the belief that the emperor was not just a military and civic leader but actually divine—was a core belief in the ancient Roman world, and the bust from the

Yorkshire horde was most likely used as an object of worship. It was discovered among other such ancient objects, which suggests that the cache was buried as an offering to the Roman gods.

The bust itself, which measures only 26 cm tall, is made of marble, and in its original form was likely painted in bright colors, like most devotional artwork of the time. The paint has since disintegrated, leaving bare marble behind. The bust shows the classically handsome head and heavily-muscled shoulders of the emperor. Like all ancient Roman art, it borrows heavily from the ancient Greek tradition...

The information was interesting and gave her a lot of background on the piece, but instead of sating her curiosity, the paper simply exacerbated it. She really should do some laundry and cleaning, and maybe make a run to the grocery store. But she itched to go to the library to do some research.

Harriet knew herself well enough to know that she'd never get anything else done when her mind was so distracted by the issue at hand. She grabbed her car keys and her coat and headed for the door. If she hurried, she could make it back in time to get ready to meet Will.

The White Church Bay Library was a charming stone building with white shutters on either side of the tall windows that flanked the door. Harriet made her way inside and breathed deeply of the comforting aroma of old books before heading to the research area. She settled in at one of the computers and pulled up the searchable newspaper archive.

Riley's paper cited an article from the *Whitby Gazette* as her source for information about when the Beresford family acquired the bust. Harriet set her parameters to search only the local paper for the terms *Beresford* and *Marcus Aurelius* then hit return.

The first link that popped up led her to a scan of an article published on October 24, 1949. LORD BERESFORD ACQUIRES ANCIENT BUST, SIGNIFICANT LINK TO BRITAIN'S PAST read the headline. The accompanying photo was grainy, but Harriet could make out a marble bust beside an older man proudly standing in front of a large fireplace with an ornate wooden mantel.

Lord Wilberforce Beresford, the Baron of Beresford, announced today that he'd purchased an ancient marble bust recently discovered in an archaeological dig in northern Yorkshire. The bust is "one of the most significant finds in modern history when it comes to learning about the local Roman settlements in the second century," Beresford claimed. He purchased the bust from the team of archaeologists who uncovered the piece, though he declined to say how much he'd paid.

Beresford, an avid historian and adventurer, has amassed quite a collection of antiques from around the world, including a ceremonial mask from the Congo, a thousand-year-old oil lamp found in Arabia, gold earrings said to have been worn by Cleopatra, and many busts recovered from ancient Greece.

"It is important to care for cultural heritage," Beresford said. "I enjoy traveling and collecting these pieces from different parts of the globe, and I rest easy knowing they will be kept safe for posterity."

However, he adds that the bust of the Roman emperor is by far the most valuable item in his collection—and not only because it was found in his own backyard, so to speak. "We now know more about the ancient citizens of Rome who once called this great land home."

Harriet didn't know how much help this article was to Riley as she wrote her paper, but the photograph that accompanied the article was a nice visual. It gave a good sense of the bust's size and appearance.

Harriet went back to the search results, but none of the other articles appeared to have anything to do with the bust. She wasn't sure how much other articles would help anyway, since none of them would be able to tell her how the piece had gotten from the collection of the baron into a lobster cage at the bottom of the North Sea.

She decided to search, instead, for any articles that might mention the theft of the Viking coins. Sergeant Oduba had told her the coins were stolen from a museum. Surely an event like that would have made headlines. Harriet adjusted her search parameters and easily found a couple of articles from the past month that appeared to be about the theft.

Viking-Era Coins Stolen from Atkinson Museum, the headline read. Harriet didn't know how she'd missed it when it came out. Then again, she didn't exactly read the weekly paper from cover to cover, so if the story hadn't been on the front page, she might very well have missed it.

Police were called to the Atkinson Museum in northern Yorkshire on Monday afternoon where a security guard discovered that a cache of coins from around the ninth century was missing. The coins had been in the collection of Count

Atkinson of Pickering and bequeathed at his death to the Friends of the North Yorkshire Cultural Society, along with the house and gardens. The coins were reported to have been discovered in 1985 when a parking lot behind a supermarket was torn up to make room for an apartment complex, and an archaeological site was uncovered.

Museum staff report that the museum, housed in the former home of Count Atkinson, was open to visitors at the time of the theft. They also report that there was a security guard on staff and that the museum has a state-of-the-art security system.

Representatives from the museum would not comment on how the theft might have taken place.

That was interesting. The coins were taken from the museum while it was open to visitors, while a security guard was on duty, and despite state-of-the-art security. So how had the theft been achieved? She read the two follow-up articles, but there was no new information. It didn't appear that the theft had been solved.

Harriet went back to the main search page and tried different combinations of search terms, but none of them yielded any new results. She made a note to herself to try to find out more about the theft at the Atkinson Museum if she could.

For now, though, she had one more thing to dig into. She searched for the name *Shane O'Grady* in the local paper.

FISHERMAN ARRESTED FOR SELLING STOLEN MUSSELS read one headline. There were plenty of others.

O'GRADY PLEADS NOT GUILTY IN MUSSEL THEFT SCHEME
O'GRADY: "HOW WOULD I KNOW?"

POLICE ARREST O'GRADY ON SUSPICION OF DAMAGING
REFRIGERATOR

SECURITY CAMERA FOOTAGE PLACES O'GRADY AT THE SCENE
OF REFRIGERATOR DAMAGE

O'GRADY PLEADS NOT GUILTY IN REFRIGERATOR REVENGE
SCHEME

O'GRADY FOUND GUILTY, RELEASED WITH TIME SERVED

As she skimmed the articles, Harriet put together that Shane
O'Grady first came to the attention of the police after several commercial mussel farmers complained that the mussels in their desig-
nated areas had been harvested by someone else.

O'Grady had hired an occasional truck driver named Richard
Long to steal mussels from other farmers and had sold them in his
shop, O'Grady's Seafood. Security camera footage placed Long's
truck at the marina, and a witness testified that he'd seen someone
matching Long's description there. When Long was arrested, he immediately told the police who'd hired him. O'Grady denied the accusation,
but bank records showed a payment from O'Grady to Long the day
before the theft. When the police searched his seafood shop, they
found coolers of mussels in the back—more than could be accounted
for from O'Grady's own fishing.

It was hardly a complicated scheme, and with no apparent
thought for avoiding detection. The second time O'Grady was
implicated, over a year later, was even worse. He was forced to close
his seafood shop, likely because of the cost of legal fees from the
mussel scheme, coupled with the fact that no one wanted to buy
from a criminal. The newspaper article about the opening of a new
store in the same building, Imperial Seafood, quoted several

customers saying how much cleaner the new shop was and how friendly the owners were.

A week later, Shane was caught on security camera approaching the outdoor electrical panel at the shop and cutting the wires. Thousands of dollars' worth of fish had spoiled. It hadn't been hard to prove that he was guilty.

Shady O'Grady indeed. Harriet could see why Martina thought he was a potential suspect. But *was* he responsible for putting the stolen objects into the lobster trap? Based on the crimes he'd been convicted of, she doubted it.

Harriet leaned back and stretched her arms over her head. She needed to get ready soon if she was going to be on time when Will got there. She logged out and pushed herself up. She'd learned a few things, and the context was helpful. But it still felt as if she wasn't any closer to understanding what had happened or how those stolen antiquities had ended up at the bottom of the sea.

She also wasn't any closer to knowing how to respond to Dustin. But she pushed that thought out of her head. She wouldn't worry about him. For now, she had a date with a man and a boat.

CHAPTER SIX

Will drove them to the marina and led her to a floating dock where a dozen boats of various sizes were tied up. Besides the hundreds of boats docked at the marina, there was a long line of cars with boats on trailers at the launch ramp.

"The people who tow their boats here," Harriet said. "Is that because they don't want to keep them at the marina?"

"Probably not," Will replied. "I bet nearly all of them are on the waiting list. It's just that spots come up so rarely, you could be waiting for forty years to get a dedicated slip."

"What?"

"The families that have them tend not to let them go," he explained. "Kyle's lucky because his grandfather got a slip decades ago. They've kept a boat there ever since."

"Whoa." Harriet couldn't imagine waiting that long to get a spot at the dock.

"There he is."

Will pointed to a white boat with raised seats for the driver and passenger and a big open area at the back. The name *Seas the Day* was painted on the side. Kyle waved to them from the driver's seat.

The boats they passed on their way down the dock varied in size and shape, from tiny speedboats to larger fishing vessels topped with satellite dishes and adorned with poles, to cabin cruisers with entire rooms beneath the deck for motoring around in comfort. There were even a couple of sailboats and one that Harriet would consider a genuine yacht.

Most of the boats were emblazoned with names, ranging from the sweet to the humorous. *Louise June. Carpe Diem. Serendipity. Odyssey. Knot Working. Shore Thing. The Unsinkable II.* She chuckled at the last one.

"You made it." Kyle hopped off the seat and moved to the side of the boat, holding his hand out to help them board. "Go ahead and step right there," he said to Harriet, pointing to a ledge on the inside of the boat lined with strips of grippy tape.

She took his hand and climbed over the side, followed by Will. The back area of the boat was scattered with towels, ropes, and other equipment. A small space at the front held life jackets and other odds and ends.

"What a beautiful night for a boat ride," Will said. "Thank you."

"It's pretty much perfect," Kyle said as he untied the ropes that held the boat to the dock. "Thank you for giving me the motivation to go out. I need to check my traps anyway, so this works well."

"How long have you been collecting lobsters?" Will asked.

"Oh, since I was a kid," Kyle said. "My dad and grandfather did it before me."

"How many traps do you have?" Harriet asked.

"I have five," Kyle said, "which is the most you can have with a recreational permit."

"And you get to keep everything you catch?"

"Well, you have to toss back any females with eggs or that are at the right age for breeding, as part of the sustainability aspect." Kyle coiled the ropes and sat down in the driver's seat. "But pretty much anything else, yeah. Some years you don't get much. Last year I only caught four all season. But some years you get almost more than you could possibly eat."

"That sounds amazing," Harriet said. Even four fresh lobsters was nothing to sneeze at. She supposed with the cost of gas and owning the boat, they probably ended up being four very expensive lobsters, but lobster was expensive in a restaurant too.

"I don't even like lobster all that much," Kyle said as he started the motor. "It's more of an excuse to get out on the water." A dull roar sounded from beneath them.

Kyle told them to take their seats, and they both sat on the ledge. Will smiled and patted his pocket then slipped his arm around Harriet, and she leaned against him. She felt safe and warm, with the wind whipping around her face and the sunshine sparkling on the surface of the water all around them.

Kyle pulled away from the dock and slowly motored out of the marina. They passed a dock with a gas pump, several rows of boat slips, and a bay for coast guard and police boats. Once they made it out of the marina, the city of Whitby, its buildings clinging to the steep cliffs that surrounded the water, receded slowly behind them.

Will asked Kyle about his work, and they chatted about his woolen shop and how much foot traffic picked up in the summer months. Once they got out onto open water, past the breakers, Kyle sped up, and the engine was too loud to hear one another talk.

Harriet enjoyed the feel of the wind in her face, the scent of the salty water, and the view of the beautiful craggy coast as it receded behind them. She could see the haunting arches of Whitby Abbey, the ruins of a seventh-century church, standing on a promontory that looked out over the sea. She could also see the buildings of White Church Bay along the coast. A few people walked along the waterfront path that linked many of the villages up and down the coast.

They passed dozens of buoys painted a myriad of patterns and colors, but Kyle kept driving. Finally, he slowed the boat and started scanning the surface of the water. "They should be right around here somewhere. Yellow and red stripes."

"That should be easy to spot," Will said.

"That's why I picked that combo. Some people pick colors from their high schools or colleges, but I just went with something that would be easy to spot. I also went with a simple alternating stripes pattern." He pointed to a group of buoys off to the right, painted with bright red and yellow stripes and contrasting sharply with the surrounding water. "Case in point."

When they neared the first one, he circled the boat around it and handed Will a pole with a large hook. "Try to grab it with this."

Will managed to hook the rope, and then Kyle indicated Will should take the steering wheel. The men changed places, and Harriet ducked out of the way while Kyle hooked the rope over a pulley and turned on the winch, which began to pull up the trap.

"Is that a new winch?" Will called.

"Got it this year," Kyle said. "It's much kinder to my back than pulling traps up by hand."

A moment later, the lobster trap broke the surface of the water, seawater streaming out of it. Kyle grabbed the wire cage and set it on the side of the boat while Will continued to circle the general area of the buoys. Kyle tugged on a pair of thick rubber gloves and opened the lid of the trap.

"Look what we have here." He pulled a large lobster out by the tail, its front claws grasping at the air. "We're in luck. This one's a male. Do you mind handing me those, Harriet?"

He pointed at a set of strangely shaped pliers and a bag of wide but small rubber bands. Harriet handed him both, and he expertly used the pliers to thread rubber bands over each of the lobster's claws. He put the lobster in a cooler then reached for another cooler marked *bait*, grabbed a handful of unidentifiable brown muck, and tossed it into the trap before closing it and unhooking the rope from the winch. He pitched the trap over the side of the boat, and they watched it sink out of sight.

"You want to steer us over to another one?" Kyle called, and Will drove to the next buoy that bobbed in the water. Kyle repeated the process, but he had to throw back a female lobster and a crab. When they pulled up the third trap, they got another large male lobster.

"That's the limit for today," Kyle said.

"You can only take two?" Harriet was surprised by this.

"Two per day. This area is known as the lobster capital of Europe but, sadly, it's been overfished," Kyle said. "The limit is part of a conservation effort."

As they motored back to the marina, Harriet considered what she'd learned in the light of the stolen antiquities. It wouldn't have been hard to drive out to the traps, pull them up, and toss in the rubber containers. There was no one around, and there were no security cameras out there. Even if someone had seen what was happening on the boat, they wouldn't think it was odd for a fisherman to pull up a trap and toss it back down into the sea.

It really was a smart idea. If someone hadn't accidentally pulled up the wrong trap, the thief probably would have gotten away with it.

Back at the marina, Will and Harriet helped Kyle clean up the boat, and then Kyle gave them the lobsters to take home.

"You don't have to give them to us," Harriet protested. "What would you have to show for the evening?"

"I don't even like lobster, remember? I got to take the boat out, which was what I really wanted." Kyle grinned. "Take them and make a nice dinner."

Will picked up the cooler. "Thank you. I'll bring this back tomorrow."

"No problem. Thanks for a great evening."

At the parsonage, Will filled a large pot with water and set it over the flame to boil.

"You think a judge will assign a worse fate to yesterday's outlaw lobster?" Harriet asked with a laugh.

Will chuckled. "I suppose it probably depends on whether it was a first offense. Maybe the judge will go easy on him, but I for one want to see justice served."

Harriet shook her head. She loved how he could always make her laugh.

While the lobsters cooked, Will chopped fingerling potatoes and garlic while Harriet made a salad. When the lobsters were bright red, he broke them down and set the pieces on plates with tiny dishes of butter and lemon juice.

Harriet forked up a morsel of the tender meat, dipped it in butter, and popped it into her mouth. It practically melted on her tongue, and she could hardly stifle a groan of pleasure.

Across the table, Will had tied a cloth napkin around his neck like a bib and grinned at her. "Not a bad way to spend an evening, is it?"

"Not a bad way at all."

He made her feel safe and happy. He made her laugh. He was godly, kind, honest, and cared deeply about others. He was everything she'd always prayed for in a man. Especially after that text from Dustin, Harriet could see how God had blessed her so richly. What had felt to her like her biggest heartbreak was really God rescuing her from making the biggest mistake of her life, and leading her to His perfect plan for her.

Before she went to bed that night, Harriet pulled up the text from Dustin and carefully typed out her response.

It's good to hear from you, and I hope you're well. But I don't think it's a good idea for you to come to Yorkshire. I hope you have an amazing trip to London, and I wish you nothing but the best.

She started to set her phone down, but then she saw that Dustin was typing a response. It was early evening in Connecticut, and he was probably still at work. The indicator that he was writing a response disappeared and reappeared a few times, but no new message came through.

She checked her phone again after she let Maxwell out one last time and then again when she settled into her bed with her book, but by the time she turned out the light, he still hadn't responded. She finally went to sleep, unsettled. She dreamed about lobsters and Roman warriors, and she was tired and groggy when the alarm went off far too early the next morning.

But those dreams had set something off in her brain, and as she dragged herself out of bed, she toyed with an idea.

CHAPTER SEVEN

T here was still no message from Dustin on Wednesday morning.
That was *good*, she reminded herself. She didn't want to be in
touch with him. That was the whole point. Still, she couldn't help
but wonder what he'd been typing the night before but never sent.

After a cup of coffee and morning devotion, Harriet got ready
for her day and left the house early. May was a busy month for a
veterinarian, and today she was scheduled to check on a colt who
wasn't growing as quickly as expected. Harriet suspected an intesti-
nal parasite, but she would need to run some tests to know for sure.

It was a foggy morning, and mist hung over the hollows like a
shawl, bathing the whole landscape in ethereal beauty. She prayed
while she drove, asking for wisdom and compassion as she went
about her day and for guidance and insight as she sought to discover
who could have registered that trap in Myles's name.

At the farm, Harriet stepped into the wellies she kept in the
boot—laughing at herself for how many Yorkshire words were
becoming part of her normal vocabulary—and treated her first
patient of the morning, a gorgeous red-gold colt with a beautiful
silky mane. She confirmed the presence of parasites and left a course
of medicine that would clear them out quickly.

On her way to the Land Rover, she checked her watch and was glad to see she had time to make a stop before heading back to the clinic. She wanted to try catching Liam Beresford at home. Even though he was a recluse, he took long walks each day along the cliffs with his dog, Coleridge, so he might not be around. Even if he was home, she didn't know whether he would see her. Lord Beresford avoided involvement with the greater community and denied most visitors, but he'd always been welcoming to Harriet.

She trundled up the long driveway lined with elms. Eventually the three-story home came into view. The stately manor was built of gold-colored stone, complete with peaked gables on both sides of the facade and dozens of mullioned windows. A circular driveway led to the house, which was surrounded by rolling green fields. There were two cars parked in the drive—Liam's Bentley and a dinged-up sedan she recognized as belonging to Mrs. Lewis, Liam's housekeeper.

Harriet rang the doorbell, and a few minutes later, Mrs. Lewis answered the door, her gray hair pushed back with a thick headband.

"Hello, Harriet. How are you, darling?" Mrs. Lewis ushered her inside.

"Hi, Mrs. Lewis. I'm doing fine, thank you." Harriet stepped inside the entry hall. "How are you? How's your daughter?"

"She's well, thank you, and my little grandson is great too. Grant told me last night, 'Grandma, when I get old, I'm going to have a red sports car.' I told him he'd better start saving his pennies now, and you know what he told me? He said, 'I'll just use some of your money.' Now, why he thinks I have any money for a sports car is beyond me. Isn't he the cheekiest thing?"

Harriet chuckled. "That's very cute. You never know what's going to come out of a kid's mouth."

"Isn't that the truth? Now what brings you here?"

"I was hoping to see Lord Beresford for a moment."

"Normally I'd send people away, but I know the baron feels differently about you. I'll see if he's available."

Harriet stood alone in the soaring entry hall while Mrs. Lewis bustled out. She gazed around the huge room, taking in the dark wood paneling, black-and-white checkered floor, and carved wood staircase.

Oil portraits of several of the former barons hung on the walls. Harriet admired them, noting how the art style and fashions changed over time, even while the individual barons' poise and carriage remained the same.

"Harriet?"

The sound of Mrs. Lewis's voice startled her. "The baron will see you. He's in his study."

Harriet followed Mrs. Lewis through the cavernous drawing room appointed with large fireplaces and rugs and drapes and into a much smaller wood-paneled study. The walls were hung with more portraits of people in Victorian dress. Curtains were thrown open to let in the light, and most of the space in the room was taken up by a heavy oak desk.

Lord Beresford sat behind it reading a newspaper, but he lifted his head and smiled when Harriet stepped into the room. "Hello, Harriet." He stood and held out his hand, and she shook it.

Coleridge, the baron's purebred bloodhound, thumped his tail against the rug by the fireplace.

"Good morning, Liam. Good morning, Coleridge." She bent down to scratch the dog's head before taking a seat in the leather chair the baron indicated.

"Did you see this?" Liam asked, gesturing at the newspaper. "About what they found in a lobster trap out in the North Sea?"

"I haven't," Harriet said. The *Whitby Gazette* came out on Wednesdays. It made sense that the news had hit the paper, but she hadn't had a chance to read it yet. "What does it say?"

He showed her the headline on the front page. PRICELESS ANTIQUITIES RECOVERED FROM LOBSTER TRAP IN NORTH SEA. "It doesn't sound like the police have many leads at this point."

"Am I right that one of those pieces was a bust that belongs to you?" Harriet asked.

"You are," Liam said. "They call it 'a priceless Roman bust from the first century, owned by the Estate of the Baron of Beresford.' Then it says, 'The baron could not be reached for comment.'" He gave her a sheepish grin.

Harriet laughed. "No surprise there."

"Why would I want everybody reading about my business?" He folded the paper and set it on his desk. "You don't seem to be surprised by the news, though you haven't read the paper. I take that to mean you're here to ask me about the bust too?"

"I heard that one of the pieces that turned up in that lobster trap belonged to you, and I was hoping you would be willing to tell me more about it."

"I can tell you what I told the police when they came here yesterday," he said, leaning back in his chair. "The piece was acquired by my grandfather, and I've never paid much attention to it. Truthfully,

I didn't even realize it was gone until the police showed up and asked me about it yesterday."

"So it wasn't in a place you normally look every day?"

"My grandfather was an avid hunter-gatherer of antiques," Liam said. "There's an entire room upstairs dedicated to his collection, and it's—well, it's a lot. Would you like to see it?"

"Yes," Harriet said. "If you don't mind, that is."

"I don't mind at all." He led her out of the study, Coleridge trotting at his side. "It's not that I don't care about the bust. Of course I care about all the things my predecessors have amassed. It's just that there are so *many* of them, and what does one do with a collection like that? I suppose you're meant to show it off, but I can't abide having a bunch of people traipsing through my home to look at some old bones and such."

"Bones?"

"There are a few Paleolithic skulls, among other oddities," he said. "Some of the collection is valuable, sure, and it probably should have gone to a museum ages ago so the public could enjoy it. But I've just never gotten around to going through everything and making a decision."

They passed more portraits of former barons, and at the top of the stairs he led her down a colonnaded hallway and into a large room. He flipped a switch, and overhead lights blinked on.

As she gazed around from the doorway, Harriet understood why he hadn't noticed the missing bust right away. At first glance, she saw a portion of a marble column, a display of early bronze tools, an African ceremonial mask, a drapery-enclosed Louis XIV bed, an elephant's foot umbrella stand, a collection of pistols in a glass case, and half a dozen gemstones in various stages of refinement, in addition to the Paleolithic skulls he had mentioned. And that was just what she could see from the doorway. It was a large room, but it was chock-full of items from different ages and places in the world.

"You're right. Your grandfather was quite the collector," she observed.

"He loved to travel, and he was from a generation that believed taking things from different cultures and bringing them to England was the best way to preserve them," Liam said. "I know these days there's a movement to repatriate this stuff back to where it came from, but I don't have the slightest clue how to do that." He gestured around the room. "As you can see, he was prolific. One of these days I should probably explore my options where these items are concerned."

Coleridge stepped forward and sniffed a stuffed pheasant on top of a black-and-red cabinet decorated with painted cherry blossoms.

"But the bust wasn't from someplace else in the world, right?" Harriet said.

"No. He was quite happy to gallivant around the world for things to add to his collection, but he collected antiquities from the UK as well," Liam said. "Those were his favorites, really. He considered the ones found here as proof of our long and storied heritage."

"The bust of Marcus Aurelius was stored in this room?" Harriet asked.

"Over here." He walked her through the room, past more artifacts than Harriet recalled seeing in most of the museum rooms she'd visited, to a side table. An empty space in the middle, surrounded by a fine layer of dust, showed where the bust had sat.

"I really don't come in here much. I find it rather overwhelming."

Harriet could understand that. "So you didn't realize the bust was missing until the police told you it was recovered?"

"I didn't," Liam said. "Although I got an email about it a few weeks ago. Someone offering to buy it. I ignored it, as I do most of my messages."

"Do you know who sent the offer?" Harriet asked.

"I don't remember. Some collector. I did come up here and check out the bust when I got the email, just to make sure I knew what he was talking about. So I know it was here then."

"When was that?"

"Early April."

"Why didn't you want to sell it?"

"Because I'd have to go to the hassle of finding out what it's worth and then dealing with the taxes, etc."

"Would Edward be upset if you sold it?" Edward was Liam's son and heir to the title of Baron.

"No. He'd rather have the cash."

"Do you still have the email?"

"I dug it up and printed it for the police when they came by yesterday."

"Would you be willing to print it for me as well?"

"Sure. I'm happy to send it to you."

Harriet looked around the room. It struck her, once again, how strange the aristocratic system was. She couldn't imagine having a house so large that she could dedicate an entire room to a collection that no one ever saw or bothered to spend time in.

That reminded her of another question. "Why, of all the pieces in this room, was the bust taken?"

"I've wondered about that too," Liam said. "Maybe because it's one of the oldest objects here, and also one of the most culturally important to the history of the UK. Plus, it's extremely valuable. I might still have some of our original land if the previous barons weren't so passionate about their collection."

"You received this mail last month, and you know the bust was here then. And you discovered it missing yesterday?"

"That's right. When the police came and told me about it."

"I guess the obvious question is, who had access to this room during that time?"

"That's what I've been trying to figure out too. But the answer is no one."

"Have you had any visitors?"

"None. No family members, no guests."

"Your sons didn't come for Easter?"

"Oh no. It's too far for Stuart to come from Canada, and Edward couldn't make the time. They all came at Christmas, and I haven't seen them since."

"What about people from the community?"

"I always say no if I can. I've gotten a few requests about it. In fact, a student emailed me a couple of months ago, asking to come see this particular bust. But I never responded."

"Riley Sloane."

He blinked at her in surprise. "You know her?"

"I met her yesterday because she's interning at my grandfather's art gallery. She's studying art and wrote a paper about the bust for one of her classes."

"That sounds right."

"Why wouldn't you let her come see it?"

"I can't abide having strangers in my house, combing through my things." He shuddered. "And now you see why. Maybe it was this student who took the bust."

Harriet didn't understand his thought process, but she knew enough to know she wasn't going to change it. He'd spent most of his life avoiding visitors, and she wasn't likely to make a difference in that now. But she did want to press him on his last statement.

"How would Riley have taken it if she was never in the house?"

"Maybe she..." He started but then stopped. "I don't know."

"What about Mrs. Lewis?" Seeing the horrified expression on Liam's face, she added quickly, "Maybe she would know if anyone's been inside the house?" She hadn't meant to imply that she thought the devoted housekeeper could be behind the theft, but it was clear that was how Liam heard it.

"I suppose she would," he said. "She's working on a list for the police of the repair people who have been inside the house recently. I'll ask her to share that with you too."

"Could I also get the email from the student?" Harriet asked.

"Of course," Liam said. He switched off the lights and ushered her back downstairs, Coleridge loping ahead of them.

"I hope you'll forgive me if I leave you here," Liam said when they got to the entry hall again. "It's time for Coleridge's walk. I'll send Mrs. Lewis to see you out."

"Thank you. Have a lovely walk." Liam was an odd duck, but Harriet knew how lucky she was to have been welcomed inside his home at all.

He nodded at her and walked toward the back of the house with the dog following. She stood waiting in the entry hall. Liam had said that Mrs. Lewis was going to see her out, but even though Harriet stood there for a few moments, Mrs. Lewis didn't appear. Should she keep waiting, or should she slip out quietly?

Harriet decided she should probably just leave, but as she turned toward the door, Mrs. Lewis came bustling in.

"Here you go," she said, holding out two sheets of paper. "The baron said you wanted the email from that student asking about the bust and the one from the person who wanted to buy it. I'm sorry for the wait, but I had to find the emails to print them."

"Thank you for chasing these down for me," Harriet said as she took the papers.

"The baron also asked me to send the list of repair people your way as well when it's ready. There are several people on it. There's always something in need of repair around here."

"I can imagine." The sheer size of the house was overwhelming. "Liam insists there's been no one in the house besides repair people. Is that true?"

"It is, at least to my knowledge. Well, he doesn't like visitors much, does he? And those sons of his only come when they want something." It was clear from her tone how the housekeeper felt about her employer's offspring.

Harriet hated to hear that but decided to leave it alone. "I look forward to seeing that list. Thank you for all your help, Mrs. Lewis."

"I'll make sure to get it to you when it's ready. It was good to see you, Harriet."

As soon as she got in her car, Harriet read the emails. The first one was from Riley, sent at the end of March.

> *Dear Lord Beresford,*
>
> *I am a student at the University of Whitby, and I'm studying art history with an emphasis on early classical influences in British art. I'm hoping to write a paper about a bust I believe is in your collection, an ancient Roman bust of Marcus Aurelius. I would so appreciate the chance to see the piece in person if that is a possibility. It would mean a lot to me and to the advancement of art history.*
>
> *Thank you for your consideration,*
>
> *Riley Sloane*

It was hard to believe he hadn't at least responded to such a polite note, but that was Liam. He seemed to have a phobia of people.

The second email was more direct.

> *Lord Beresford:*
>
> *I am an expert antique dealer based in York. I'm working with a private collector who is interested in acquiring your Marcus Aurelius bust. If you are willing to part with the piece, I could get you a great price. Please let me know at your earliest convenience.*
>
> *Mason McGinnis*

Mason McGinnis. Where had she heard that name before? Harriet started the Beast's engine, still running the name through her mind. As she shifted into reverse, she remembered where she'd seen it. It was in some paperwork she'd found in Grandad's files. If she wasn't mistaken, Mason McGinnis was an art dealer who had sold some of Grandad's work years ago.

Before she could think too much about it, she put the car back in park, pulled out her phone, and called Ida. "Hi, Ida. It's Harriet. Do you know a Mason McGinnis?"

"Oh yes," Ida replied. "He's an antiques dealer mostly, but I've run into him a few times over the years, as he sometimes sells artwork as well. He sold some of your grandfather's pieces long ago, before the gallery was set up, I believe. Why do you ask?"

"I think he was trying to buy the bust that was stolen and ended up in the North Sea."

"What?" Ida squawked.

"I have something that indicates he was trying to get ahold of it before it was stolen."

"Well, if he was, I'm sure it was all honest and aboveboard. Mason is a good man."

Harriet filed this information away and drove back to the clinic, still trying to process Liam's room of treasures from around the world. Why was that particular bust taken? Who had taken it, and how did they gain access? And how did it end up at the bottom of the North Sea?

She would need to answer those questions later. She had patients waiting.

CHAPTER EIGHT

Good morning," Polly said when Harriet walked into the clinic. "How was the colt?"

"He's gorgeous," Harriet said. "And after a short course of dewormer, he'll be nice and healthy again."

Polly glanced at the wall clock. "You must have stopped somewhere on the way back from the farm."

"I did. I thought our first appointment today wasn't until ten."

"You thought right. Ringo Starr will be here soon."

"Ringo Starr?" Harriet chuckled.

"His namesake cat," Polly clarified. "This Ringo is an elderly tabby."

"What a great name for a cat."

"Right now, I want to know what you found out. I know the reason you didn't get back sooner is that you were doing research for this lobster thing."

"You know me too well." Harriet laughed. "I stopped to talk to Liam Beresford."

"How'd you manage that? Lord Beresford doesn't really do visitors."

"I know, but he has a soft spot for my family, so he let me in."

"And?" Polly tapped her pen on the desk impatiently.

"He showed me the place where the bust should have been." Harriet told her more about the visit and about the email from Mason McGinnis.

"So do we think Mason McGinnis came in and took it when Lord Beresford said he wasn't going to sell?" Polly mused.

"Haven't the foggiest," Harriet admitted. "I do think an art dealer sneaking into the house to steal a bust seems a bit far-fetched. And Ida says the guy is totally aboveboard. But I don't know. *Someone* got in and stole it."

"So when are we talking to Mr. McGinnis?"

Harriet noted the *we* and smiled. "I haven't the slightest idea."

"Let me do some research," Polly said. "It looks like our first patient is here."

A middle-aged man stepped inside with a howling cat in a cage—no doubt the fabled Ringo Starr. The name didn't sound too far off.

Harriet spent the rest of the morning seeing patients, including several dogs, a couple of cats, and one tiny kitten getting its first shots. She caressed the top of the curious little ginger's head and handed it back to its owner then felt her phone vibrating in her pocket. She checked it as she walked out of the exam room.

Dustin was calling.

She silenced it and quickly returned the phone to her pocket. She certainly wasn't going to answer that right now. She was at work.

Harriet was planning to go to the kitchen and grab something quick to eat, but Polly apparently had other ideas. "Mason McGinnis has a shop in York."

"He does?"

"Yes. And it's open this afternoon," Polly said with a pointed expression.

"Too bad we have patients all afternoon."

"We don't. Your last appointment of the day was at three, but Mrs. Blabey had to cancel, which means we're done at two thirty. Now we have plenty of time to run over to York."

"Why did she cancel?"

"She had a family emergency, so she rescheduled her dog's annual checkup for tomorrow." Polly consulted her phone. "I've mapped it out, and if we leave right at two thirty, we can get to York, talk to Mason, and make it back in time to visit the Atkinson Museum before it closes."

"We can?"

"You were going to talk to someone at the Atkinson Museum to find out about the Norse coins stolen from them, weren't you?"

"I suppose I was. I hadn't really thought that far ahead yet." Harriet didn't have any reason not to go through with the plan Polly had sketched out for the afternoon if they would be done so early. "So we'll leave right after our last appointment."

Harriet went to the house to make a quick sandwich, noting that her kitchen cupboards were starting to look mighty bare, and came back in time to see Noodle, a tan-and-white cat with a thyroid condition, and then Junkyard, a teacup chihuahua with an ear infection. By the time the last patient was gone, Polly had cleaned up the office, shut down her computer, and slung her purse over her shoulder.

"Are you okay to drive? Angus dropped me off this morning," Polly said. Angus was the younger of Polly's two older brothers.

"That's fine with me," Harriet said.

They climbed into the Beast. Polly programmed the address into her phone's navigation app, and soon they were on their way. As was so common with good friends, lively conversation filled the drive, and before long they reached York.

Harriet parked in a lot on the outskirts of the city, and they made their way across the river into the old town, whose skyline was dominated by York Minster, a towering Gothic cathedral. They walked down the narrow streets and alleyways—called Snickelways in this city—that were lined with timber-framed Tudor facades and ancient brick shops. Eventually they found the address of Mason McGinnis's antique shop and art gallery, housed in a row of beautiful stone buildings. The gallery was sandwiched between a high-end jewelry shop and a classic tearoom.

They stepped inside the shop and found themselves surrounded by intricately carved beds and dressers and curio cabinets and sideboards and other items Harriet couldn't even name. All she could see was that the furniture was very ornate, with lots of scrollwork, swirls, and feathers etched into wood polished to a high sheen, and that the attached price tags had several more digits than she might have expected.

"Whoa," Polly said, taking in the cascading chandeliers and crystal vases from another era. "Do people actually pay that much for this stuff?"

"I suppose they must," Harriet said. Shops like this were where rich people outfitted their country homes with period antiques, though such furniture was out of fashion with people her age.

"Can I help you?" A man appeared from the rear of the store. He wore a dapper dark suit with a purple tie and pocket square. She guessed he was in his midfifties, with graying brown hair and dark-framed glasses.

"Hello. I'm Harriet Bailey, and this is Polly Thatcher," Harriet said. "We were hoping to speak with Mason McGinnis."

"I'm Mason," he said. "What can I help you with today?"

He wasn't originally from Yorkshire. Harriet could tell that from his accent. It sounded Irish, which she supposed would make sense, given his last name.

"We're from White Church Bay," Polly said. "We wondered if we could ask you about some antiques that were recently found in Whitby, just up the coast."

"I'm intrigued. What kind of antiques are we talking about?"

Harriet expected a flicker of recognition or something else to indicate that he'd heard about the situation already, but there was nothing of the sort. He genuinely seemed to be curious about what they had to say. Did he really not know what antiques they were there to talk about?

"Specifically, we want to ask you about a bust of Marcus Aurelius that dates to Roman times," Harriet said. "It was in the collection of Baron Beresford."

His eyes widened. "Is he interested in selling it? Pieces from that time can be quite valuable if they're in decent shape."

Was he trying to feign ignorance? "He's not interested in selling it. I thought I should confirm that for you, since you emailed him about it recently."

"I what?" His mouth dropped open. "No, I didn't. I've never heard of the piece until just now."

"Perhaps you've forgotten, but you did email Lord Beresford to see if he was interested in selling the piece. I saw your letter myself."

"Let me be clear. I never emailed anyone about a Roman bust. I wouldn't forget a find as significant as that. But I can assure you I'm not familiar with either Lord Beresford or what's in his collection."

"That's strange." Harriet pulled the email out of her purse and handed it to him. "The proof is right here."

Mason's lips moved as he read the printout, and then he lifted his head, his brow furrowed. "This isn't from me. I didn't send it."

"Then how is it from your email address?" Polly asked, pointing at the paper.

He shook his head. "It's not. That's not my email. My email address uses my first and middle initials, MT, and my last name, McGinnis. The address here uses my first and last name. That's not me."

"Are you sure?" Harriet asked. Realizing how silly that sounded, she added, "I mean, of course you're sure. I'm sorry. You know your own email address."

She wanted to believe he was lying. But she got the sense that he was as confused by the situation as they were.

"I didn't write this," he said again. "I would never say 'a great price.' That's not how I talk about these things. And I would never refer to myself as an 'antique expert.' That's so crass, isn't it?"

"It is," Harriet conceded.

Mason handed her the page. "Besides, I was in Italy when this email was written. I spent the winter in Venice, and got back two weeks ago. I know that doesn't mean I couldn't have sent the email, but I didn't know about this piece, so I couldn't have written anyone about it."

"It's not hard to set up a fake email account," Polly mused. "Anyone could do that."

"They must have borrowed my name for legitimacy," he said.

"But who would do that?" Polly asked.

"Someone who wanted Lord Beresford to think he was selling the bust to a real antique dealer," Harriet said.

"And when that didn't work, the person resorted to theft," Polly said.

"Someone pretended to be me and then stole the piece I was allegedly asking for?" Mason's eyebrows went up.

"It would seem so." Harriet watched him carefully, but he betrayed nothing but surprise.

"Oh dear."

"Fortunately, it's been recovered," Harriet added quickly. "We're just trying to figure out what happened."

"I wish I could shed some light on the situation," Mason said. "But it has nothing to do with me."

Which meant they were back to square one.

CHAPTER NINE

I think he was telling the truth," Polly said as soon as they were back in the car.

"That's the sense I got as well," Harriet said. "And it would line up with what Ida told me about Mason being trustworthy. She didn't think there was any way he could be wrapped up in this."

"It's likely she was right," Polly said. "But it also appears that someone posed as him."

"Someone was trying to get their hands on the bust," Harriet agreed, "and decided to try impersonating a respected dealer to get Liam to trust them."

"I wonder if there's any way to trace who set up that fake email account."

"The police may be able to, so we'd better let them know about this development." It didn't sound like the police had been around to talk to Mason yet, and this was the kind of thing they would definitely want to know. "Do you want to call Van?"

"Sure." Polly checked her watch. "But let's go to the museum first and see what we can find out. It won't be open much longer."

"That makes sense."

"Great." Polly programmed the museum's address into her phone, and soon they were on their way back to the countryside.

After fifteen minutes, they turned off the main road and onto a narrow country lane that wound over a bridge, past a glen of trees, and then along a small lake. Eventually they found the black iron gates with a sign that read ATKINSON MUSEUM.

At the end of a long driveway stood a three-story Georgian-style brick house. It wasn't as large or as grand as Beresford Manor, but it was still a beautiful home. They parked in the lot and made their way inside, where a woman at a desk collected their entry fee and gave them brochures about the museum's collection. Walls of books and trinkets and postcards were for sale all around her.

"Sir Richard Atkinson was an art lover, and he amassed one of the most extensive collections in the Yorkshire region," she said proudly. Her white hair was pulled back into a tight bun, and she had heavy bifocals and a pinched face. "He loved Renaissance and Victorian art, as well as more primitive artifacts, and you'll see both on display inside the museum. When he passed, his home was given to the trust and this museum was established to share his wonderful collection with the public. Please let me know if you have any questions."

"We will," Harriet promised, and they took the brochures and wandered into the museum.

The first gallery to the left must have once been the drawing room, with its high ceiling and long drapes and large fireplace. Now its walls were painted stark white and hung with paintings of military battles. Soldiers in red coats stormed battlefields. Judging by the kilts the opposite side wore in one of them, Harriet guessed the painting represented one of many skirmishes with the Scots to the north. Harriet scanned the rest of the paintings, all military scenes, before they moved on to the next room, which was filled with gold-leafed backgrounds and one-dimensional portraits of Mary and baby Jesus.

"It's so interesting how painting has evolved over time, isn't it?" Polly observed.

Harriet agreed, and they made their way to the next room, where there were paintings of men and women in colorful clothes cavorting around open fields of what might have been ancient Greece.

As they wandered through galleries, Harriet looked around to find where the security cameras were placed. There were cameras in most corners, and they met a guard in a gallery of objects from India, Australia, Fiji, Hong Kong, and Bermuda. The guard, a young man in a black uniform, stared down at his phone and didn't even glance up when they entered the room.

Eventually, they found their way to the rear of the house and to a small gallery that was dedicated to ancient items. There was a glass display case featuring several metal tools, including one labeled Bronze Age Knife. Harriet wondered how they'd determined that, but she trusted that the experts knew what they were talking about. There were probably all kinds of methods for dating ancient items, and people who studied them regularly could likely also figure out what they'd been used for.

There was a collection of other pieces of metal that were described as jewelry, and a life-size re-creation of a fur-and-skin garment that the placard said was typical of Bronze Age clothing.

In the middle of the room was an empty display case with a forlorn label that read, Norse-era coins, circa 800 CE. Thin wires snaked up from the base of the pedestal to the glass-walled case.

"They were right here in the middle of the room," Polly said. "That's bold, isn't it? It's wired and everything."

"And there are cameras in two corners," Harriet said, nodding toward them. "Plus a guard wandering the galleries."

"Though all signs point to that not being much of a deterrent," Polly said. "He didn't seem particularly attentive when we saw him."

"Still, I wonder how the thief was able to get the coins out of here without detection. It happened while the museum was open, so he must have gotten around the security system somehow."

"How about we ask the woman at the front what she can tell us?"

"Good idea. I doubt we'll be able to figure out anything else by ourselves here."

They made their way back through the galleries to the front of the museum.

"Did you have any questions?" the woman asked.

"Nothing about the collection itself," Harriet said. "Though we were hoping you might be able to tell us more about an incident that happened here recently."

"We're told there was a theft last month," Polly said. "We were wondering if you could tell us anything about that."

"I cannot," she said, her voice cold. Tiny muscles around her mouth twitched, and she shook her head. "I'm afraid I am not at liberty to discuss anything about that. Do you have any questions about the collection itself?"

Harriet looked at Polly. This woman wasn't going to budge, and frankly she couldn't fault her loyalty. "We don't. Thank you for your time," Harriet said.

They walked out to the car.

"At least we got to see the place," Polly said, pulling open the car door.

"I don't know about you, but that's simply raised more questions for me," Harriet said. "I don't understand how a thief was able to get those coins out undetected in the middle of an open museum with all that security."

"Do you think it was an inside job? Like maybe the thief was working for the museum?" Polly suggested. "If they knew how to shut off the alarm on the display case and get rid of any security camera footage, plus when to do it to avoid the guard on his rounds—"

"Assuming he ever made any rounds," Harriet said. "I wonder how many people the museum employs. It can't be more than a handful."

"And I'm sure the police questioned them all thoroughly," Polly added. "Still, maybe that's why the woman at the front can't talk about it, because one of the employees is suspected of the theft."

"Maybe it was her," Harriet said with a grin. It seemed so unlikely that the dour elderly woman was behind it that it was almost funny. Then again, maybe that was how she'd managed to get away with it. "But it's probably more likely that she's refusing to fuel the grapevine."

Harriet was about to start the engine when something moved in her peripheral vision. She turned her head and saw the museum guard walking toward them. She rolled down her window to see what he wanted.

"Hi, sorry, but I heard you asking about the theft that happened here a few weeks ago. Midge refuses to talk about it, but she's on the side of the museum and thinks Oscar Ramirez did it, which is ridiculous. If you want to hear his side of the story, you should talk to him."

"Is Oscar the guard who was on duty when the theft occurred?" Harriet asked.

"Yes, but he didn't have anything to do with it. No way. I know him—he would never do something like that. But Midge and the owners are determined to believe he did it."

"Do you know how we could get ahold of Oscar?" Polly asked.

"Yeah, we've been close mates since school. He's working at Sorenson's, the clothing store at the shopping center, because the museum sacked him after the theft. I'm meeting him to watch the football game after he gets off work, so I know he's there today."

Initially, Harriet was puzzled by the idea of a football game in June, but then she remembered that nearly everywhere in the world, football was what Americans called soccer.

"Thank you," Polly said.

The guard gave them directions to the shopping center. "Tell him Gabe sent you." He glanced over his shoulder at the museum. "I'd better get back."

"Thanks, Gabe," Harriet said. "It was good to meet you."

He nodded and hurried away.

"Well, that was helpful," Polly said. "Much more so than the woman at the desk."

"She was just doing her job," Harriet pointed out. "To be fair, I would hope that Ida wouldn't spread gossip about the gallery. Should we make a stop at the shopping center before we head back?"

"Definitely," Polly said. "It's in the right direction."

The shopping center was located on the main road and resembled a lot of other shopping centers Harriet had seen. There were some stores they didn't have in the States, but for the most part, she could have easily been back home in Connecticut.

They parked and found their way to the big chain clothing store. Inside, they were greeted by blasting pop music and racks upon racks of clothing in all kinds of bright colors and patterns.

A man in a black suit who stood by the door nodded to them as they entered.

"Hello," Harriet said, smiling at him. "I'm looking for Oscar Ramirez. Is he around?"

"That's me," he said. "Can I help you?"

"Did you used to work at the Atkinson Museum?" Polly asked.

"Yes?" He seemed uncertain.

"I'm Harriet, and this is Polly. We were just at the museum, and Gabe said you might be able to talk to us about the theft of those coins a while back. We want to hear what happened from your perspective."

He scowled. "Are you reporters?"

"No," Harriet said.

"Why do you want to know then? Are you with the police?"

Would it help to tell him they were trying to prove that an elderly fisherman was innocent? She doubted it. He might become another person who wanted Myles to be guilty. She decided it was best to deflect. "Just busybodies, really."

"Gabe says the museum is trying to pin it on you but that you had nothing to do with it," Polly added. "We want to hear your side."

He considered that for a moment. "I have my break in ten minutes. I'll meet you around back, by the dumpsters."

"Great. We'll see you there."

Harriet and Polly walked down to the end of the long strip of stores and followed the sidewalk around to the rear of the shopping center. There were a few cars parked there, and at the end of the row were the dumpsters.

"Charming spot," Polly said.

"Yes, well, at least there isn't loud music playing," Harriet said, shaking her head. "I don't know how anyone can stand to be in there for long."

"There he is," Polly said as Oscar came out the back door of one of the shops and walked toward them.

"Thanks for meeting us," Harriet told him.

"I want to set the record straight with as many people as possible," Oscar said. His dark hair curled around his face, and he shifted from one foot to the other. "I don't know who took them, but it wasn't me."

"Why don't you tell us what happened?" Harriet suggested. "But first, how long did you work at the museum?"

"About six months. My mate Gabe started there first, about a year ago. His uncle worked there for a while before that. Gabe took over for his uncle and said it was a good job, so when they were hiring another guard, he recommended me."

"And was it a good job?"

"I mean, it was easy. It's not an extremely popular place, so you don't have to deal with that many people. You sweep the galleries once an hour, and other than that, you can pretty much be left alone. But in some ways it was really bad."

"How?" Polly prompted.

"The security is a total joke, but I didn't realize that until I'd been there a while."

Harriet was surprised, given all the cameras she'd seen. "What do you mean?"

"For one thing, they have all these display cases that are wired as if they're alarmed, right? They look like if you touch them, something bad will happen." Oscar folded his arms over his chest. "But they don't work. They never have, as far as I know."

"The display cases aren't protected?" Harriet couldn't believe it.

"Nope. All the wires are for show. You can open the cases, and nothing will go off. Which is exactly what happened when those coins were taken. And there are all kinds of cameras around, but half of those don't work either."

"Are you kidding?" Polly sounded as stunned as Harriet felt.

"I wish," Oscar replied grimly.

"So there wasn't any footage of the theft then?"

"There was some," Oscar said. "One of the cameras in that room actually worked. You can see a guy stealing the coins, and it's very clearly not me. But they decided I had something to do with it anyway. They think I told him about the fake alarms and the one camera that does work, because he was careful not to let that one catch his face."

"You've seen the footage?" Harriet asked.

"Yes, but I don't have a clue who the guy is. I've never met him, I wasn't working with him, and I have no idea how he knew about the alarms or the camera."

"Do you know where we could get a copy of that footage?" Harriet asked.

"I suppose you would have to ask at the museum, but I doubt they'd agree to let anyone see it without a warrant. All I know is they said I should have stopped him. There are twelve galleries in that museum, and only one guard working at a time. How am I supposed to see what's happening in all the galleries at once?"

"Where were you in the museum when the theft took place?" Polly asked. "And how did they discover the theft had happened?"

"I was in the Renaissance room at the end of a sweep," Oscar said. "There's a chair there that's out of the way, and I can sit there between rounds and keep an eye on things. You can see it on the footage. I went through the Primitive Room at 3:07, and there was no one in there. When I came back to the room on my next round, the coins were gone. I called one of the owners, she called the police, and that was that. They fired me the next day. It wasn't my fault, but when a theft happens on your watch, that's the end of your job as a guard."

"Do you think the thief was watching you, waiting until you'd done your round for the hour before he went in and took the coins?" Harriet asked.

"I think he must have. The timing was too good for it to be random."

"And how would he have known when you were going to do your rounds?" Polly asked.

"My best guess is that someone must have told him—the same person who told him about the security camera and the alarms on the display cases."

"Do you think maybe he could have watched until he discerned a pattern?" Harriet asked.

"It's possible, but I don't know. He had to know about the security lapses somehow, and I doubt he could have figured that out from simple observation."

"Who do you think told him?" Polly said.

"Well, it wasn't the guards, I can tell you that. But there are half a dozen volunteers who staff that place, and any of them could have been the one to tell him."

"Can you think of anyone who would have wanted to get their hands on those coins?" Harriet asked. "Any of the volunteers?"

"Who's to say?" Oscar replied. "But are the police talking to the volunteers? No, they're fixated on the guards."

Harriet wondered how much stock to put in this opinion. Was there any truth to the idea that the volunteers weren't trustworthy? "So none of them has done or said anything that makes you think they might be involved?"

"No one sticks out." He snorted. "Besides, they were just a pile of metal. I honestly can't imagine why anyone would want them. I know they say they're old and that makes them valuable, but I don't see what the appeal is."

"Do you know anything about a bust of Marcus Aurelius?" Harriet asked.

"Who?" His brow wrinkled.

"He was a Roman emperor. Have you ever seen a bust of him?"

"I don't think there was one of those at the museum, was there?"

"No," Harriet said. "I was just wondering."

"Oh. Okay." He glanced at his watch. "Anyway, I've got to go back in. My break is almost up."

Harriet smiled at him. "Thank you for using it to talk to us."

"I hope they find the guy, whoever it is. Then they'll see it wasn't me."

They thanked him and got back in the car.

"So?" Harriet said as she pulled out of the parking lot. "What did you think?"

"It sounds to me like Oscar truly doesn't know what happened," Polly said. "And that the security at the museum is spotty at best—nowhere near as secure as they've led the public to believe. But it also sounds like he's not taking any responsibility for the fact that this happened on his watch."

"It does seem kind of impossible for one guard to be able to see the whole museum at one time," Harriet pointed out.

"True, but if the guards only patrol the rooms once an hour, it doesn't seem like it would take a genius to figure out the pattern and know when it would be safe to steal the coins. Especially if they knew that the case wasn't hooked up to an alarm and which cameras don't work."

"Someone must have told the thief about those things," Harriet agreed.

"So the thief must be someone who works there or someone who knows someone who does."

"Or someone who spends a lot of time there, figured out the guards' patterns, and picked up on the security flaws."

"Right. So checking out the people who work or volunteer there might bring something to light. And we need to get our hands on that security camera footage."

Harriet grinned at Polly. "If only we knew someone with a connection at the police department."

Polly laughed. "I'll see if I can convince Van to let us see the footage."

"Don't get him in trouble or anything."

"I won't. He won't give it to me if he shouldn't." She adjusted the air vent. "I'm starving. Have you talked to Shady O'Grady yet?"

"I haven't," Harriet said.

"Then let's kill two birds with one stone. How does dinner at the Crow's Nest sound?"

Harriet didn't really have any plans. She'd intended to get to the grocery store, but talking to Shane was more important. "You think he'll be there?"

"I think he's there nearly every night, so chances are good. You need to meet him anyway. He's a local character."

Harriet put the Land Rover in reverse. "Let's go."

CHAPTER TEN

Harriet decided to stop at the house and let Maxwell out before they went to the Crow's Nest, and Polly agreed. "It'll give me a chance to call Van."

As Harriet climbed out of the Beast, Riley stepped out of the gallery with a young man and waved at Harriet.

"Hi, Harriet." Riley tugged the guy toward Harriet's car. "This is her," she said to him. "Harold Bailey's granddaughter, the one I told you about." Then she said to Harriet, "This is my boyfriend, Johnny Bradley. I told him about you yesterday."

"Hello, Riley." Harriet smiled. She stepped forward and held out her hand. "It's very nice to meet you, Johnny."

"It's great to meet you too." His voice was deep, and he had dark hair and high, strong cheekbones. He and Riley looked like they belonged together. "Riley was very excited to talk to you about that old bust."

"It's not just an old bust," Riley said, hitting him playfully on the arm.

Harriet gestured for Polly to step out of the car then made introductions.

"It's very nice to meet you both," Johnny said. "Enjoy your evening."

The young couple walked toward a small blue car parked in front of the gallery.

"I'm going to run in and take care of Maxwell," Harriet said. "It'll just take me a minute."

"No problem." Polly returned to the car.

Harriet went inside and let Maxwell out. When she brought him back in, she refilled his food and water, as well as Charlie's. She patted both animals and trotted out to the car.

Polly was staring down at her phone when Harriet got into the Land Rover.

"Care to hear something interesting about Johnny?" Polly asked as Harriet backed out of the parking space.

"Riley's boyfriend?" Harriet put the car in gear and drove forward. "Are you cyberstalking him?"

"I wouldn't say that. I figured I'd look him up, since I had a minute. He's a senior at the university."

"That makes sense, since Riley is there too."

"But she's doing art or something, right? Johnny is studying marine biology."

"Okay." Harriet had gone through a marine biology phase once, when she'd thought she wanted to spend her life swimming with dolphins. "Am I supposed to find that suspicious? You said it as if it's significant somehow."

"He currently works at the marine research center at the university. In a lab that's studying lobsters."

"What?"

"Their website says Yorkshire is the lobster capital of Europe. Due to overfishing and changes in the ocean's currents, the lobster population is way down, so this lab is working to study and eventually repopulate the lobsters in the area."

Harriet was starting to see what Polly was getting at. "So he works with lobsters, and she studies ancient art."

"Exactly. It's a bit fishy, isn't it?"

"More crustacean-y, if you ask me."

Polly made a face. "I will not dignify that poor attempt at a joke with a response."

"Oh, come on, that was funny," Harriet said. "Anyway, I see your point. She knows a lot about ancient art and artifacts, and he knows about lobsters."

"One would assume, given where he works."

"But she was so excited to talk to me about that bust, and she didn't seem weird when she introduced him to us. If they were in on it together somehow, wouldn't Riley be avoiding me?"

"Who knows what she would be doing?" Polly said. "I don't understand how criminals think."

"We don't know that they're criminals.'

"No, but it does merit further investigation, don't you think?"

"Yes. But for now, dinner."

The Crow's Nest was a pub filled with dark wood booths, worn wooden tables, green glass hanging lamps, and a roaring fire even on this late-spring day. It felt comfortable and homey.

Polly led Harriet inside and pointed to a booth in the corner of the room, where a rail-thin man sat alone, picking at the remains of a burger and fries and staring down at his phone. "That's Shane."

Harriet studied the man, who wore stained jeans and sneakers with an oversize sweatshirt.

"Let's grab that table there," Polly said, pointing to a small table next to his booth.

"Great."

When they were settled, Harriet scanned the menu board and saw that the special was steak and Stilton pie, which sounded delicious.

Polly caught her eye then pretended to notice their neighbor for the first time. "Shane O'Grady? Is that you?"

He looked up from his phone and squinted at her. He had a few days' worth of graying stubble across his chin.

"Polly Thatcher," she said. "My dad is Alex Thatcher."

His eyes widened. "Oh, wow." He gave her an obvious once-over. "You've grown up, haven't you?"

"I have. Happens to the best of us. Oh, this is my friend Harriet Bailey."

He nodded. "You're Doc Bailey's kid, the one that took over for him?"

"Harold Bailey was my grandfather, but yes, I took over his practice."

"Your grandfather was a good man," he said. "He used to treat my poodles before they passed."

"We miss him."

"And I work with Harriet at the clinic," Polly said. "How are you doing?"

"All right. Keepin' busy."

"Are you still fishing?" Polly's Yorkshire accent came on strong.

"Most days. I had to start over with my shop, but I'm close to getting enough together to open in a new location."

"That's wonderful. I remember the old shop fondly. For my mum's birthday dinner last year, we went and got her lobsters. She picked out the one she wanted, and Dad cooked it for her. She loved it." And then her eyes widened, and she said, "Wait. I read something about lobsters in the paper this morning. I didn't really understand it, but you're the perfect person to ask. I can't believe we ended up sitting right here next to you."

"I don't know anything about those lobsters in the paper," Shane said sharply. "If that's what you're talking about. People keep asking me whether I put stolen art in some lobster trap. Now let me ask you, why would I do something like that? I don't know anything about art. What kind of moron would put art in a lobster trap anyway?"

"Now that's a good question," Polly said with a laugh. "That's what I don't understand. Like, isn't it meant to be valuable stuff? That's what the paper said. But if it's so valuable, what was it doing at the bottom of the sea?"

"Some harebrained scheme to smuggle it out of the country, from what I gather," Shane said. "And the police think I'm involved."

"Why would they think that?" Polly demanded.

"Prejudice. Everyone always thinks if something fishy happens, I must be involved, but I had nothing to do with this."

"Fishy?" Polly laughed. "I get it."

It took him a minute to understand, and then a smile broke over his face. "Clever. Just like your dad." He took a drink and set his glass back down. "But again, I had nothing to do with this. I'm on probation. The last thing I need is more bad press, especially when I'm about to open the new store. People avoided shopping at the last one for months after—well, for a while."

Polly frowned. "Oh yeah. Wasn't there a dustup about oysters or something?"

"It was mussels, and I didn't know where Richie got them," Shane said. "He showed up with them, and I bought them. How was I supposed to know he took them from someplace he shouldn't have?"

That contradicted what the newspaper reported, that Richard Long claimed Shane hired him specifically to get the mussels. Harriet decided to keep that to herself.

"Plus, my wife moved out after—well, there was an incident last year where I was unfairly maligned in the press, and my wife couldn't take it."

Harriet guessed that was about the time he'd cut the wires to the refrigerator.

Shane's face brightened. "She's starting to talk about moving back in. I wouldn't risk that by doing something stupid now."

"So why do people think you were involved with the lobster thing in the paper?" Polly asked.

"Because people aren't very creative," he said. "Whenever something happens with seafood around here, people assume it must be Shady O'Grady again." So he was aware of the nickname. "But this time, it wasn't me. I've learned my lesson and turned over a new leaf."

"You're Not-So-Shady O'Grady now?" Polly grinned.

A smile spread over his face in answer. "Never was Shady O'Grady, but sure. In any case, I hope they find whoever did it, because the police have already been at my door twice to question me, and I'm just trying to live my life. It's becoming harassment."

"So you never applied for a lobster permit this year?" Polly asked.

"Of course I did, but a commercial one that lets you take out more than two at a time. I'd go belly-up if I could only sell two lobsters a day."

"Do you know who Myles Stafford is?" Harriet asked.

"I know of him. Nice old guy, from what I understand. But I didn't use his name to try to get a recreational permit or whatever the police seem to think I did. I keep telling people I'm a new man, but no one believes me. They want to pin this on someone, and I'm a convenient option."

"That must be frustrating," Polly said. Then she tilted her head, as if an idea had occurred to her. "Who do you think did do it?"

Shane seemed to consider. "Not a commercial fisherman, that's for sure. When you're out there every day, you see how unpredictable the sea is. The currents change, and the waves move things around. If a good storm snapped the lines and some beachcomber took the buoy that washed up on shore for their 'seaside serenity' collection, that valuable treasure would be lost forever at the bottom of the sea. It had to be one of those day-tripper types. Someone who has a boat because they think it's cool to serve lobsters they caught themselves but has no idea what the sea is actually like."

"Do you have any guesses?" Polly asked again. "Anyone who comes to mind?"

He hesitated and then said, "Could be any of them. I don't know. There are so many of them these days. Plus, my wife says I shouldn't cast aspersions. She says it's unattractive. I'm trying to be better about it. So no, I don't know."

"How is Carol doing?" Polly asked blandly, as if idle gossip had been her aim the whole time.

Shane answered with a long tale about how she'd moved back in with her mother—who had allegedly never liked him and took every opportunity to remind his wife of that—and how their adult children sided with their mother in the separation. He talked until Polly and Harriet's food arrived, along with his own bill.

He rose from the table. "I should get going. But thank you for speaking kindly to me this evening. Not a lot of people do these days, though I understand why. Say hello to your father for me, will you?" He strolled away.

Harriet turned to Polly. "That was impressive."

"What was?"

"Your little act there."

"I wasn't acting. I mean, I did play dumb a few times to get him to talk about the lobsters, but mostly that's just how I am with people from around here. Small towns and all. So what did you think?"

"He seemed genuine in insisting his innocence," Harriet said. "But he also said he was the victim of bad press when it came to the refrigerator thing."

"Even though he was caught on camera doing it," Polly added.

"And he denied responsibility for the stolen mussels, though the account in the paper says he hired Richard Long to steal them," Harriet said. "So I think it's safe to say he's not totally reliable."

"You're right about that," Polly said. "But still, I kind of believe him about this."

The difficult thing was, Harriet did as well. Which meant that their prime suspect had just moved down the very short list, and she wasn't sure who else to put at the top.

In her jacket pocket, her phone buzzed. She pulled it out and glanced at the screen to find a text from Dustin.

MY FLIGHT TO LONDON LEAVES FRIDAY NIGHT. I'D REALLY LIKE TO TALK WITH YOU WHILE I'M IN ENGLAND.

"What's wrong?" Polly was too astute sometimes.

"What do you mean?"

"Don't try to fool me, Harriet. You're grimacing at your phone. Someone you don't like?"

"Not exactly. Well, kind of."

Polly set her fork down. "Now I'm intrigued."

"It's Dustin. He's coming to London, and he wants to come up here to talk to me."

"Oh my goodness." Polly grabbed Harriet's forearm. "He wants you back. He's coming here to beg you to give him another chance."

Was he? "I don't know. Maybe."

"How good will it feel to tell him you've moved on, and send him packing?" Polly crowed.

Harriet shushed her, unable to muster the excitement Polly obviously felt.

"Wait. You *are* going to send him packing, right?"

"That's probably not even why he's coming."

"Wait. What about Will? You aren't really going to get back together with Dustin, are you?"

"Never." She said it more emphatically than she needed to. "I'm not sure I even want to see him again."

Polly's tone changed to one of sympathy. "Too hard?"

"No, that's not it." Truly it wasn't, but Harriet didn't know how to express what she was feeling. "I've moved on. I've healed. I just don't want to see him. I have this feeling that it'll complicate things somehow."

Polly nodded. "It's totally up to you whether you want to see him again. But maybe it would be good for you to do it, so you could see how he stacks up against Will and get closure on the whole thing once and for all. I haven't met him, but I know he can't compete."

"Will is a really good guy," Harriet said.

"Half the women in town were after him before you got here. You have no idea how many hearts you broke when you snatched him up."

Harriet snorted. "They were not."

"Were so," Polly insisted. "You're lucky you didn't get your tires slashed and your windows broken. There were women all over town crying into their tea the day you showed up and turned his head." She reached out and placed her hand on Harriet's. "And since that day, Will's only had eyes for you. He loves you, and he's a good, kind, honest man."

Whether or not the part about other women was true, Harriet knew Polly's last statement was. Will was exactly the sort of man she'd been looking for. The kind of man she knew her parents were praying for her to find. She loved Will. Her heart had moved on.

"I told Dustin I didn't think it was a good idea for him to come," Harriet said.

"Suit yourself," Polly said with a shrug. "Maybe it's small of me, but I'm sad to miss the chance to meet him and see him realize what a big mistake he made. And I still think it would be good for you to get that closure."

As they went back to their meal, Harriet had to wonder if Polly was right.

CHAPTER ELEVEN

Harriet dropped Polly off at home and headed to Cobble Hill Farm. She was exhausted from the long day, but she was also on edge, so she was happy to see her aunt sitting in her garden. Dr. Genevieve Garrett—Aunt Jinny—ran a family medical practice out of her dower cottage, and having family so close was a blessing as Harriet got settled in her new life.

She took a seat next to her aunt at the little table among the blooms. The roses perfumed the air with their sweet scent, and iris and delphinium brightened their beds.

"Would you like some tea?" Aunt Jinny sipped from a beautiful porcelain cup.

"No, thank you," Harriet said. "But I wouldn't mind sitting for a moment. It's lovely out here."

"Nothing beats a spring evening," Aunt Jinny said. "Have you had a nice night?"

"Yes, it was good. Polly and I had dinner at the Crow's Nest."

"That's nice. Good to see you two getting out together."

"Well, we had an ulterior motive. We wanted to talk to Shane O'Grady."

Aunt Jinny's eyes widened. "Shady O'Grady? Why did you want to talk to him?"

"He says he's turned over a new leaf. He's Not-So-Shady O'Grady now."

Aunt Jinny laughed. "That'll be the day."

"You don't believe him?"

Aunt Jinny took another sip from her cup. "I suppose the Lord can change any heart. But failing divine intervention, I wouldn't trust a word that comes out of his mouth."

"He appeared earnest about trying to change though."

"That doesn't mean he wasn't lying through his teeth."

He'd said some things that didn't add up, but Harriet thought he'd sounded credible at other times. She knew she couldn't trust everything he said, but did that mean she couldn't trust any of it?

"Was your sudden interest in Shane motivated in some way by the story in the paper this morning about that art found in a lobster trap?" Aunt Jinny asked.

"It was."

"I figured. If something shady happens down at the marina, it's a safe bet that O'Grady's involved."

"We don't know if he is though," Harriet said. Shady or not, she didn't want to assume he was involved if he wasn't.

Aunt Jinny studied her in silence for a moment then said, "You should talk to Matilda."

"Who?"

"The bowl that was found belonged to my friend Matilda Chetwood. Or it was hers, until she sold it recently."

"You're friends with the person who owned the Neolithic bowl?"

"I'm friends with pretty much everybody around here. If you want to talk to someone, just ask."

"I didn't even know the name of the person who owned the bowl. I didn't get that far." The name hadn't been in the newspaper article.

"Well, it was Matilda. We've been in a book club together for years, and she texted me today saying the police came by to talk to her. They were accusing her of trying to smuggle antiquities out of the country or some such nonsense. It was very upsetting for her."

"What did they say to her?"

"That the bowl was probably meant to be picked up by someone who intended to take it out of the country. But she didn't know that. She simply sold it to the man who wanted to buy it, and she didn't think anything of it until the police showed up at her door."

"Wait. How did she happen to have a bowl from the Stone Age in her possession to begin with?"

"Oh, there are all kinds of things in attics around here." Aunt Jinny waved her hand dismissively.

Given the things Harriet had seen in Liam Beresford's home and the Atkinson Museum, she didn't have a hard time believing her aunt. But this piece would have been *really* old.

"She had an item from the Stone Age lying around in her attic?"

"I think it belonged to her father, but you should get the details from her. I'll send you her number." Aunt Jinny pulled her phone out of her pocket and swiped at the screen. A moment later Harriet's cell dinged. "I'll let her know to expect you to be in touch."

"Thanks."

Harriet asked Aunt Jinny about her day, and her aunt told her a funny story about a child who'd come into the clinic for annual shots. Then they chatted for a while about Aunt Jinny's son, Anthony, and his family. Finally, when the shadows were starting to gather around the edges of the garden, Aunt Jinny picked up her cup and said it was time to head in.

"You go ahead and give Matilda a call," she said, patting Harriet's shoulder. "And tell me what she says."

"I will."

Harriet headed back to her own house, where she unloaded the dishwasher and folded some clothes. Then she decided it wasn't too late to give Matilda a call. People her own age hated receiving calls out of the blue, but Harriet suspected Matilda was of a generation that welcomed them.

Her call was answered on the second ring. "Hello?"

"Hello, this is Harriet Bailey. Is this Matilda Chetwood? My aunt, Jinny Garrett, gave me your number."

"Ah, yes, she told me you'd be calling. She said you wanted to hear about the bowl?"

"Yes. I was hoping you could tell me a bit more about it, such as how you found it and what happened with it."

"Right. Well, maybe it would make sense for you to visit my dad's place so you can understand why I sold it. Can you come by tomorrow?"

"Let me check." Harriet quickly reviewed her schedule for the following day. "Where is your dad's place?"

"On Peacock Row in the village. Do you know it?"

"I do. I can be there around lunchtime, if that works for you."

"I'll see you then." Matilda said goodbye and hung up.

As Harriet set her phone down, she thought about Dustin's latest text. She really should tell Will about it, but he was leading a Bible study, so she couldn't call him. She needed to take Maxwell out and get to bed. It had been a long day, and there would be another one tomorrow.

But her mind raced with questions. Who had applied for a lobster permit in Myles Stafford's name? Who impersonated Mason McGinnis and emailed Lord Beresford about the bust? Who came into Liam Beresford's house to steal the bust? Did someone at the Atkinson Museum manipulate the lax security to take the coins? Was Shane O'Grady really turning over a new leaf? There were so many questions, so many things that didn't make sense.

But there was one lead in particular that Harriet was eager to look into. It was probably nothing, but it would give her something to do that would hopefully help her wind down.

She opened up her laptop and typed the name *Johnny Bradley* into a search engine. It was a common enough name that she had to do some sifting, but it wasn't too hard to find the right Johnny on social media. Unfortunately, his profile was private, so she couldn't see any of the photos he'd posted.

Back on the main search page, she found an article he'd written for the student newspaper, arguing for higher pay for adjunct professors. She found a photo of him on the high school basketball team. He was originally from a town called Masham. That was interesting enough, but none of it was especially useful.

She looked up the website of the University of Whitby Marine Research Center. It wasn't hard to find, and she browsed the page.

The center was part of the Biological Sciences Department. It was headed by a Dr. Jacob Brunner, who specialized in marine mammals. The center was "a valued part of the university's legacy of research and advancement of knowledge." And...*finally.*

The center had its own social media, which showed Harriet something very interesting indeed.

CHAPTER TWELVE

Harriet didn't have any early-morning appointments scheduled for Thursday, which was good because it had taken her quite a while to fall asleep the night before. She'd been too excited by what she'd seen on the marine research center's social media and spent some time trying to figure out how she might learn more about Johnny Bradley. Finally, she came up with a far-fetched idea that might actually work. Sometime after that, she was able to fall asleep at last, and she was grateful for the extra hour of sleep in the morning.

After she got dressed, she took her coffee and her Bible to the table on her patio and let Maxwell run around the yard, his little wheels squeaking behind him, as she read more from Acts about the cities Paul traveled to and the churches he helped establish in them. The man who had so recently persecuted Christians was now a missionary, spreading the good news of how his life had been changed. She couldn't help but think of Shane O'Grady and hope that he'd also found a new direction for his life.

Refreshed, she cleaned up the kitchen and got ready for her day. Polly wasn't in the office yet when Harriet stepped through the door to the clinic, so she flipped on the lights and got things set up for their first appointment.

Polly burst in a few minutes before eight. "I'm so sorry I'm late," she blurted. "Angus was supposed to drop me off, but his car wouldn't start, and I ended up riding my bike."

"You're not late," Harriet assured her. "We open at eight, remember?"

"I know, but I like to be here early to set up so you don't have to," Polly replied.

"It's really okay," Harriet insisted, though she was disappointed that she didn't have time to tell Polly what she'd seen the night before.

The morning flew by, and soon it was time for their lunch break and her visit to Matilda Chetwood.

"I have to run out for a meeting with my aunt's friend, who apparently sold that Neolithic bowl. Do you want to come along?"

"Of course I do, but I have to cycle home and wait for the tow truck, since Mum has to leave." Polly wrinkled her nose. "I told Angus I had to be back here by one, so don't worry about that."

"I'm not worried," Harriet said. "Just disappointed you can't come with me."

"You'll tell me everything that happens, right?"

"I'll give you a full update," Harriet promised. "By the way, if you have a moment, you should check out the social media posts from the University of Whitby Marine Research Center."

"You can't just say something cryptic like that and then leave," Polly protested, but Harriet laughed and walked out the door.

She got into her car, drove to the parking lot in the upper part of town, and then walked down the steep steps that led to the lower, and older, portion of White Church Bay.

She would never get over how charming the village was, with its golden-colored stone buildings pressed right up against one another, its narrow streets and alleyways, and its unique shops. The whole town seemed to spill downhill toward the boat launch that let out to the beach, where for generations the villagers had set off in their boats. The boat launch wasn't used for much besides tourist photos these days, but it was still chock-full of character.

Harriet made her way to Peacock Row, which was little more than a paved path where fishermen's cottages were pressed right up against one another. The byway was lined with beautiful old stone houses, and she found the address Matilda had given her easily enough.

A woman with gray hair waited for her outside a blue door. She wore a light trench coat and pumps, and Harriet was impressed that she could manage to walk in them over the uneven cobbled paths.

"You must be Harriet," she said. "I'm Matilda. It's nice to meet you."

"Thank you for agreeing to see me," Harriet replied, shaking her hand.

"Of course. I'm so upset by what's happened. I had no idea—I didn't realize I was doing something wrong in selling Dad's things. But come, you'll see." She unlocked the front door and pushed it open.

Harriet stepped inside what must have once been a quaint fisherman's cottage, with wooden beams on the low ceilings and white paneling on the walls. Harriet was sure there was furniture in the room somewhere, but it was hard to see it because every surface was cluttered with stuff.

Ceramic figurines of all kinds covered the coffee table. Bowls, pitchers, and vases crowded together on a side table and a set of built-in bookshelves. Stacks of books and magazines were piled on the couch, with more stacks on nearly every square inch of the floor. Harriet wasn't sure there was a path through the room, even if there had been anywhere to go. From where she stood, she could see into the kitchen, which was similarly piled with stuff.

"Dad was a collector," Matilda said. "At least that's what he always called it. A doctor might call it something else, but having his things around him made him happy. We never tried to curb his habits, though maybe we should have." She picked up a ceramic figure of a woman dancing and gave a sad little laugh. "Believe it or not, I've already sold a lot of what was in here."

"I can see how such a task might be overwhelming," Harriet said.

At least there wasn't any visible garbage or anything. Matilda's father seemed to be a man who had loved beautiful things.

"There was a bowl from the Stone Age in here?" Harriet asked. She couldn't understand how such an important record of early civilization could have been kept in a place like this.

"Dad owned many strange things. The bowl was part of a collection he received when a friend of his passed many years ago. I think it originally belonged to the friend's grandfather or something. I remember him telling us how old it was, though we didn't believe him. I guess he was right, though I didn't learn that until the police talked to me. I have no idea why such a valuable item was privately owned rather than in a museum."

"How did you end up selling the bowl?"

"I listed it on an auction site a few weeks ago."

Harriet tried to hide her horror at the idea of a Stone Age bowl in an online auction, but she must have failed.

"You have to believe me—if I'd known what it was, I would have made sure it went to a museum where it belongs," Matilda said. "My dad thought all this stuff was valuable, but most of it is pretty worthless. I did suspect that I might be able to get money for some of it, so I gathered up the things he thought were worth the most and listed them online."

"So you didn't want to take them to an auction house or find an antiques dealer to sell them?"

"I have no provenance for any of it, and I wasn't sure how long it would take while the pieces were investigated for authenticity. The online way is so easy and so fast. We're still paying the mortgage on this place while we're settling the estate, and David—that's my husband—said the sooner we get the things out the better. I was so happy when I got a bid on the bowl right away."

Harriet wasn't surprised it hadn't taken long. "Did you know anything about the bidder?"

"Does anyone really know anything about who buys their stuff online? I didn't even think to ask. No one else bid on it. After I got it ready for shipping, I looked him up and found out he was an antiques dealer. I did wonder if maybe I could have gotten more for it after all, but it was too late by that point."

"Where did you send it?"

"To a post office box in Whitby. I was so glad it was close, because it meant it would get there quickly and be less likely to break in transit. After that, I didn't think a thing of it until I saw that photo in the paper yesterday."

"Is that how you found out the truth about the bowl?"

"Yes. I saw the article and recognized the bowl immediately from the photo. When I read where it ended up and what happened with it, I called the police. They came right over yesterday and grilled me about why I was trafficking in antiquities and all sorts of crazy things." Matilda ran a hand over her face. "I couldn't believe it. I had no idea the buyer meant to smuggle it out of the country, and in a lobster trap of all things."

"I'm sorry that happened," Harriet said. "I imagine they were quite interested in the buyer."

"They were. I gave them everything I had, but it was just an email address and the post office box number."

"Would you be able to give those things to me as well?"

"I don't see why not," Matilda said. "Hang on." She pulled out her phone and tapped the screen a few times. "I kept a screenshot of the auction page, with the buyer's information. I'll send it to you."

A moment later, Harriet's phone buzzed with the incoming text. She was hardly surprised to see that the buyer was the alleged Mason McGinnis. The accompanying email address was the same one used by the person who had reached out to Liam Beresford about selling the bust of Marcus Aurelius. That explained how those two pieces ended up together in the lobster trap, at least.

But who was posing as Mason McGinnis? And where was that person now?

CHAPTER THIRTEEN

As Harriet drove back to the clinic, her phone rang. It was a number she didn't recognize, but she took a chance and answered it on her hands-free setup.

"Hello, Harriet? This is Myles Stafford."

"Oh, hello, Myles."

"I just wanted to check in and see if you've had any luck finding out who registered that trap in my name."

"I can promise you I'm working on it," Harriet said. "I have a few leads, nothing definitive. But I won't give up until I find that answer for you."

"Thank you. I so appreciate it."

He was such a nice man. She really wanted to figure this out for him.

Harriet made it back to the clinic in time to update Polly on what she'd learned with Matilda and the night before in her online searching.

"So whoever is posing as Mason McGinnis is our man," Polly said.

"Probably, though we don't have a way to tie him to the theft at the museum," Harriet said.

"Yet."

"It does seem likely there's a connection there somewhere. We just need to find it."

"It's Johnny. It's got to be. You saw this." Polly gestured to her screen, which showed the image Harriet had found on the marine research center's social media page. The photo showed a man pulling up a lobster trap in the North Sea, and the caption underneath identified him as Johnny Bradley. The photo was dated Sunday, the day before the artifacts were found in the trap. And the kicker was that the buoy in the photo was navy blue and orange, with the same pattern of colors as Miles Stafford's.

"I don't know if it's proof, but it does seem to be an indication that we need to look at Johnny a lot more closely," Harriet agreed.

"I'd call it proof," Polly insisted. "Now the only question is whether we should go straight to the police and tell them, or find out more about Johnny Bradley first?"

"I plan to do both, actually. But I'm not sure the best way to go about it. I thought of asking Riley to put me in touch with Johnny. But if Riley and Johnny are working together—"

Polly's eyes widened. "As in maybe she handles the art side and he handles the lobster side."

"Right," Harriet said. "I'm afraid it would scare her off if I asked her to connect me to Johnny."

Polly thought for a moment, tapping her pen on the counter. "I think you should do it," she finally said. "Riley knows about the find, right?"

Harriet nodded.

"You could tell Riley you want to learn about lobstering here and see how it differs from in Connecticut, and you could ask her if

Johnny would be able to introduce you to someone who could tell you more."

Harriet realized this was probably the best plan. "Do I have time to run over to the gallery?"

Polly checked her screen. "Elizabeth Hayward and Benny aren't here yet, so I imagine if you're quick, it would be all right."

As Harriet walked across the parking area, she wondered what sort of animal Benny was, but she would find out soon enough. She pushed open the door of the gallery and found Riley sweeping the floor and Ida in the back, typing at a computer. There didn't seem to be any customers at the moment.

"Hi, Harriet," Riley said brightly.

"Just the person I was hoping to see. I have a question, and I was wondering if you could help me."

"I would love to if I can." Riley appeared open and genuine, but Harriet wondered if that would change when she heard the question.

"I'm still thinking about the art found in that lobster trap."

"Oh my goodness, me too. I've practically thought about nothing else," Riley said.

Harriet believed her, though she wondered why Riley would be so fixated on the discovery. Was her interest merely academic?

"I would love to learn more about how the art could have ended up in the trap," Harriet explained. "So I want to talk to someone who knows a lot about this kind of thing. I happened to see that your boyfriend works at the marine research center at the university, and I was hoping he might be able to put me in touch with someone who could tell me more about lobsters."

"Totally," Riley said. "Johnny actually knows a lot about lobsters himself. It's one of his specialties, actually."

"What a coincidence." Or was it, as she and Polly suspected, more than a coincidence? "Would you be willing to put me in touch with him?"

"Sure. Or I can call him and see if he can show you around the center."

"That would be great." Her request was received better than she had imagined, but Harriet couldn't help but wonder how genuine Riley's enthusiasm was. If she and Johnny *were* involved in the art heist, would she be so willing to help? She might, so as to throw Harriet off their scent and see what she knew.

"I'll give him a call on my break, and then I'll text you and let you know what he says."

"Thanks."

Harriet went back to the clinic and met a woman carrying a cat carrier. Benny was a cat then.

The next few hours were busy, but when Harriet was able to check her phone again, she found the promised text from Riley.

JOHNNY IS AT THE CENTER UNTIL 5 TODAY. CAN YOU MEET HIM THERE?

The clinic closed at four, so that should give her plenty of time to make it. She sent back a message confirming that would work for her.

Polly couldn't come along, as she and Van were going to a movie. But she offered to clean and close the clinic so Harriet could get on her way as soon as their last patient was gone, and make it to the marine research center in plenty of time.

Harriet hadn't been to the university campus before, but she navigated the Gothic buildings easily enough. She found that the marine research center was housed in a new six-story building made of glass and steel that felt totally out of step with most of the campus. DeMenna Science Center, read the words above the door, and the directory by the elevators revealed that the building held labs and classrooms for many scientific disciplines. The marine research center was located on the first floor, and Harriet easily made her way there.

She opened the door and entered a large room with a concrete floor and steel counters all around. The air was tinged with the scent of saltwater, and the walls were covered with pictures of crabs, lobsters, and various kinds of fish, as well as a couple of sharks and anemones. Various doors branched off the main lobby area. Just as Harriet was starting to wonder where to go, a door opened, and Johnny stepped out in a lab coat.

"Harriet. Good to see you." She was struck again by his strong cheekbones and boyish good looks.

"Hi, Johnny. Thanks for meeting me."

"It's no problem. Riley said you wanted to learn more about lobsters, and this is the best place to do it. What specifically did you want to know?"

Harriet couldn't very well tell him she wanted to know whether he'd put stolen art in a lobster trap. "Maybe you could tell me more about what you do here at the center, for starters?"

"Of course. Come on back." He indicated she should follow him. He led her into a room off the main area. It was lined with metal shelves and counters, some with plastic bins on top. Several large glass tanks in the middle of the room were filled with lobsters of various sizes. One small tank had only one lone lobster in it.

"That's our hero right there," Johnny said, gesturing at it.

"Hero?" Harriet echoed, puzzled.

"That's the lobster that had the coin stuck in it," Johnny said. "The one you rescued."

It was identical to any other lobster to her untrained eye, so she would have to believe him. "How did it end up here?"

"The police thought it should be kept around, in case they needed it for evidence or anything like that, so they brought it here and asked us to look after it."

"That makes sense. I don't suppose there are many better places to leave it."

Johnny grinned. "We'll keep her safe. We named her Maeve."

"That's a fine name for a lobster." Maeve moved her claw, and Harriet could almost imagine she was waving at her. "Hello, Maeve."

"Okay, so you may have heard that Yorkshire is the lobster capital of Europe," Johnny began.

"I have heard that," Harriet said.

"Well, a few years back, the local lobster population was significantly down from what it was supposed to be, from overfishing, warmer waters than they were used to, and a bacterial infection that affected a large percentage of the population."

Harriet knew shellfish could get sick, but she hadn't really thought about what impact that might have. "So you're working to bring the population back?"

"Ideally. Dr. Brunner, who runs this lab, is the world's leading expert on bacterial infections in European lobsters, and his research has been instrumental in recovering the population. He cooperates with the government and fishing industries to work toward a more sustainable future for lobsters. Their recovery will prove essential to the maintenance of our current ecosystem."

"Wow. That's impressive." Not only that, but anyone who cared that much about lobsters was worth paying attention to. "I would love to meet Dr. Brunner. Is he around?"

"Unfortunately, he's on sabbatical. He's been in Costa Rica since February, studying freshwater shrimp."

"That doesn't sound like much of a sabbatical." It did mean that he couldn't be behind the thefts. It probably also explained why the police called her instead of the local lobster expert to remove the coin.

Johnny shrugged. "At least it's warm."

Harriet walked forward and peered through the glass of the tank in front of her. About a dozen lobsters swam and crawled around inside. "How did you get interested in lobsters?"

"Oh, I've always loved the sea. My family goes scuba diving in the Caribbean every year, and I've been certified since I was young. So I knew I wanted to study something to do with the ocean, and for a long time I thought I would focus on the octopus. They're smart enough to solve puzzles, and their ability to camouflage is incredible. But when I read about Dr. Brunner's reputation and his work to restore the lobster population, I knew I wanted to be a part of it. Lobsters aren't as intelligent, but they're every bit as fascinating."

It was pleasant to hear a university student so passionate about shellfish research. Then again, she supposed it wasn't all that different from the passion that had driven her to become a veterinarian, except that she was fascinated by land-dwelling animals instead of lobsters. Maybe if she'd grown up scuba diving, things might have been different for her.

"Scuba diving seems to have set the tone for your entire career."

"Oh, yeah. I've seen some incredible things." He pulled his phone out of his pocket and scrolled then handed it to her. "This is from our trip to Indonesia last year. Isn't that reef gorgeous?"

She took in the photos of a coral reef covered in every color she could imagine, and several that she couldn't. "I've never seen anything like it."

"If you scroll, you'll see some of the most beautiful parrotfish. We also saw tortoises and several kinds of sharks."

As Harriet scrolled through the pictures, a text popped up from someone saved in Johnny's contacts as DMan. BRO, I NEED THE HOUSING MONEY TODAY. IT'S TWO WEEKS LATE. MY PARENTS CAN'T COVER US AGAIN.

She kept scrolling through the photos and stopped on a picture of a tortoise in crystal-clear turquoise waters. She had to admit it was stunning.

Another text popped up from the same contact. I ALSO NEED THAT TWO HUNDRED QUID YOU OWE ME. I'VE GOT TO PAY MY PHONE BILL. SOMETHING'S GOTTA GIVE.

Harriet skimmed a few more photos then handed the phone back. "I can see why you love it. But I'm guessing there aren't too many tropical fish in the North Sea."

He laughed. "No, not many."

"So what do you do here in the lab?" Harriet asked.

"I'm still an undergraduate, so mostly I do whatever I'm told," Johnny said. "I check the pH level in the tanks, feed the lobsters— that kind of thing. I'm also responsible for going out to check the traps every other day."

"What traps?" Harriet asked.

"Oh, we have dozens of lobster traps set up out in the North Sea, where we're testing various types of bait and different conditions in the wild. It's my job to go out there, count the lobsters we caught, record the data, and reset the traps."

"So you always go to the same traps?"

"Yes," Johnny said. "Dr. Brunner's traps are to the south because the currents there are the most interesting."

"Is that anywhere near where the trap was found with those antiquities inside?"

"No, it's actually quite a distance from there," Johnny said. "Those were north while ours are south. But how crazy was that? I've never heard of anything like that happening. Dr. Brunner is so upset he missed it."

"It was pretty crazy," Harriet said. "Have you ever been out that way, to where that trap was found?"

"Sure, I've been all around this area. I mean, I get to use the center's boat, so sometimes I cruise a bit. There are some beaches you can only get to by boat, so I take advantage of that sometimes, when things aren't too crazy in the lab. But I haven't been able to do it recently. I've been chockablock with Dr. Brunner gone."

Harriet thought about how to word her next question and decided to be up front. However he responded, it would tell her something. "I ask because I saw a picture of you on the center's social media the other day. You were out checking traps."

"Oh, really? I didn't see it. Yeah, Emma came out with me last week. She handles that kind of stuff."

Harriet pulled up the photo on her phone. "Here it is. I thought it was interesting that those buoys are orange and blue, like the buoy that marked the trap where the art was found."

Johnny hesitated, then blurted, "What? No way. That's impossible." He stared at Harriet's phone, his brow wrinkled. "Ah, I see. They do appear orange in this photo, but that's because of the filter Emma used. But they're actually red and blue, the University of Whitby colors." He gestured at the university banner on one wall, which was indeed deep blue with red letters. "Our buoys are red and blue. That's them, I promise." He handed back her phone.

Harriet squinted at the photo. Was he right? Now that he pointed it out, the water and the sky seemed to have a more greenish tinge than they probably should have had in the photo. But could a filter change the color that much? The red of the buoys really did appear orange.

His phone buzzed. More messages from his roommate? But Johnny smiled as he glanced at the screen. "Riley's here. She has to pick up a book from the Archaeology and Art History department library and wants to meet up." He typed something into his phone.

Harriet understood that she was being asked to leave. Did Johnny really have to go meet Riley? Or had Harriet gotten too close to the truth?

"Riley says she'd love to see you," Johnny added, his voice flat. "Do you want to walk over with me?"

Harriet eyed him, trying to read the situation. Was Riley exactly what she seemed—a happy-go-lucky young woman excited to meet new people? Or was there more to it? Was Riley hoping to find out what had happened during this meeting and what Harriet knew? Harriet wanted to believe that Johnny was telling her the truth, but his suddenly stilted manner, his denial about the color of the buoys, and the money problems that his texts revealed, coupled with Riley's knowledge of ancient art…

"Sure," she said. "Lead on. I'm not familiar with this campus."

Johnny led her out of the lab and through the lobby of the modern building. They crossed a grassy quad and made their way up a hill toward a Gothic-style building.

"This is beautiful," Harriet said as they passed through an archway and into an area surrounded by more Gothic buildings. "What are those?"

"Dorms." Oh my. She must have really offended him with her suspicions.

"Do you live on campus?"

"Yes. My parents live too far away to make it practical to commute."

At least that tracked with what she'd seen on his phone.

"These are the classrooms. The art history department is up that way," Johnny said as they walked into another open quad area surrounded by more Gothic-style buildings of golden-brown stone. There was a tower at one end and an open colonnade that ran around the inside of the quad. It reminded Harriet of photos she'd seen of Oxford.

Johnny led her through a tall wooden door built into one wall. Inside, they found Riley chatting with a man who wore trendy dark sneakers and a button-down with the sleeves rolled up. He was tan, and his exposed forearms were well muscled. He was probably a little older than Harriet, if she had to guess, with dark hair and thick-framed glasses. He smiled a greeting at Harriet and Johnny.

"Oh good, you came!" Riley beamed at her. "I wanted to introduce you to Dr. Russell."

This was Dr. Russell? When Riley had mentioned him before, talking about all the work he'd done with museums and such, Harriet pictured an older gentleman with elbow patches and a pipe. But this man was not that.

"He's my adviser, the one the police consulted on the art that was in the lobster trap. He knows more about this stuff than anyone." Riley gestured toward Harriet. "Dr. Russell, this is Harriet Bailey. She's the veterinarian the police called to get that coin out of the lobster shell."

"I'm very happy to meet you." Dr. Russell stepped forward and shook her hand, his brown eyes warm and welcoming.

"And I'm happy to meet you," she said. "All I really did was some minor crustacean surgery. You did the hard work of identifying the importance of the artifacts."

Dr. Russell laughed. "I don't think there's anything minor about doing surgery on a crustacean." Then he cocked an eyebrow. "What did you think of our antiquities?"

"I don't know much about them, but I'm impressed by what I've heard," Harriet said. "Though it was a strange place to store them."

"Yes, I agree. Five stars for the objects themselves, but only one for ambiance. Would not recommend." He laughed. "Did Riley tell you she wrote a paper on one of them? And spent last summer in

Norfolk on a dig helping excavate a site with remains from Neolithic times?"

"What?" Harriet turned to Riley. "You were on a dig?"

"Yeah, it was really cool," Riley said.

Harriet felt her heartbeat speed up. Why hadn't Riley mentioned the expedition? She'd told Harriet she didn't know much about Neolithic times, but if she'd been on a dig and helped excavate artifacts from that time, she must know a little more than not much. So now Harriet knew that Riley had knowledge of not one but two of the time periods represented among the artifacts.

"Heinrich Bettler, one of my colleagues from Cambridge, is working on a massive project up there, and each summer I try to send some of my best students," Dr. Russell went on, apparently oblivious to the sudden awkwardness. "Riley got glowing reviews from the team in Norfolk, and she wrote a bang-up paper about the kinds of tools and objects households would have had in Neolithic times."

"I can't believe you didn't tell me that," Harriet told Riley. "That's incredible."

"I learned a lot," Riley said. "For one thing, I learned that I prefer studying in a library as opposed to digging in piles of dirt all day. I found dirt in my ears for weeks after I got home."

Dr. Russell smiled. "Fieldwork isn't for everyone. But you did help advance our knowledge of what life was like during the Stone Age here in England, and that's a huge deal."

Riley shifted uncomfortably, but he didn't seem to notice. Harriet appreciated how open he was about his student's accomplishments, though she wondered why the student herself hadn't been so forthcoming.

"Anyway, I have to run. It was very nice to meet you, Harriet." Dr. Russell drew a business card from his pocket and handed it to her. "I hope we can keep in touch. Please let me know if you'd like to discuss those artifacts further."

"I look forward to it," Harriet said, tucking the card into her pocket.

Dr. Russell nodded to all of them then ducked out into the quad.

Harriet left the university with more questions than she'd started with but even more convinced that Riley and Johnny were wrapped up in the theft somehow.

Now she needed to find proof.

CHAPTER FOURTEEN

Harriet had just walked into her house when her phone rang with a call from Liam Beresford's housekeeper. She answered immediately. "Hi, Mrs. Lewis."

"Hello, Harriet. I went back over the manor records for the past few months, and I found the names of everyone who has been inside the house."

"Great," Harriet said. "Hang on, let me grab something to write with." She rushed into the kitchen and found a pen and a small notepad. Charlie, who was sitting on the counter, watched her with curiosity. "Okay. I'm ready."

"Back in March, a chimney sweep came in to take care of the chimneys."

"A chimney sweep?" Harriet hadn't realized that was still a profession.

"Of course." Mrs. Lewis's voice was stern. "And if you haven't had yours done recently, you should. In these old houses, soot builds up in the chimneys and can lead to all kinds of problems. You should call this guy."

Mrs. Lewis read off his name and number. Then she said, "There was a plumber in early April, when the kitchen pipes got backed up.

I don't think he ever actually left the kitchen, so I don't see how he could have stolen that bust, but I'm giving you the complete list."

"I appreciate that."

After giving Harriet the plumber's name and contact information, Mrs. Lewis said, "There was also a carpenter who came to repair some woodwork around a window that got damaged during a winter storm. And then we had an exterminator when the baron heard animals scampering around in the attic." She gave Harriet their information as well. "Finally, there was a man from the Heritage Commission who came to inspect the woodwork repair to that window."

"The Heritage Commission?"

"They come around every so often, especially after work is done to the exterior of the house. We have to make sure any repairs that can be seen from the outside are as authentic to the time period as possible, and the Heritage Commission checks to make sure the rules are followed. It's all a part of making sure no one does anything horrendous to one of these old homes and ruins the character of our area."

That sounded quite onerous, but Harriet supposed it probably wasn't all that different from the rules some homeowner's associations had back in the States. "Do you have his name and number for me?" she asked.

"His name was David. I didn't get a last name. The number is on their website, I'm sure."

Once Harriet recorded all the information, she thanked Mrs. Lewis and stared down at the list. She would start making calls in the morning.

But there was one person she needed to contact right away. She'd started feeling guilty that she hadn't let Van know what she'd discovered over the past couple of days. Polly had told him about the fake email letter sent to Mason, but he hadn't been updated since then. So she took the time to call him and fill him in on what she'd learned, starting with the same person buying the bowl from Matilda, continuing on to the Atkinson Museum's security problems, and finishing with her suspicions about Johnny Bradley and Riley Sloane.

Van waited patiently until she finished then said, "Polly told me about someone setting up a fake account to email the baron."

"Right," Harriet said. "Mr. McGinnis doesn't know a thing about those emails, and the address they were sent from isn't his. And Matilda can't be blamed for assuming she was corresponding with the real Mason McGinnis."

"We've taken her off our suspect list," Van told her. He was quiet for a moment, and Harriet could hear the faint scratching of a pen in the background. "Now about this university couple. If you're right, she's the brains and he's the brawn. Is that what you're thinking?"

"Not exactly. Just that she knows about ancient art, and he has the knowledge and the means to get the art into the lobster trap."

"Noted," he said. "Thanks for the tips. We'll be sure to follow up on all of this. I don't suppose it'll do me any good to ask you to stop poking around. Smugglers tend to be serious people, Harriet."

"I'll stop poking around," Harriet said.

"Great."

"When Myles Stafford's good name is cleared," she added.

Van groaned.

Harriet grinned as she hung up, but she felt unsettled. She'd given the police what she knew, and they would handle it from there. Yet she still couldn't get her mind to relax. She tried calling Will, but he texted that he was finishing his sermon and would call her back when he could.

She could go for a walk before it got too dark. She could finally go to the store so she could make something for dinner beyond the frozen Indian dish or plain spaghetti with melted cheese.

But she knew her mind would only settle if she did her best to find answers. She refilled her pets' dishes, popped the frozen meal into the microwave, and sat down in front of her laptop.

First, she pulled up the home page of the Atkinson Museum and searched the site for any information about its staff and volunteers. The board of directors comprised half a dozen members, and they all seemed to have plenty of experience in the art field, plenty of money, or both, based on what she could tell. There was no information about the guards or the volunteers who worked there, probably for privacy reasons.

She thought back. The guard at the museum had said the woman at the front desk was named Midge. But what was her last name? And was Midge her given name, or was it short for something else? She tried a few half-hearted attempts to search for Midge online, but she didn't get anywhere. She would have to try to find out more about the volunteers another way.

She turned her attention to something else. She typed the phrase *Neolithic dig Norfolk* into her search bar. She had to refine her search a couple of times, adding the name *Heinrich Bettler*, but eventually she was able to pull up information about the dig on Cambridge's website.

She learned that Dr. Bettler was a professor of archaeology, working on a multiyear project to excavate what appeared to be ruins from before 5,000 BCE. This, according to the site, placed it squarely in the Stone Age, or Neolithic period. She also saw that each summer, Dr. Bettler welcomed student volunteers from around the UK to work on the project. She thought again about how Riley would have known the value of the bowl, since she'd been involved in the dig.

Did she know anything about the Viking-era coins?

It wasn't looking great for Riley, especially since there was that photo of Johnny on the boat pulling up a lobster trap with a buoy that was awfully similar to the one marking the trap where the artifacts were found. Was his explanation about the filter changing the colors in the photo legitimate?

Harriet went back to the social media site for the marine research center and pulled up the photo of Johnny again. Were those buoys orange and blue, or red and blue? It was so hard to tell.

If only there was a way to remove the filter on the photo, so she could see what color the buoys really were. There must be a way, but even though Harriet was a digital native, she wasn't into computers and tech enough to know how to find it. She needed someone younger. Someone who knew more about computers and social media.

Then she realized she just might know someone who fit the bill.

Harriet slept fitfully Thursday night and was still exhausted when the alarm went off Friday morning. She rolled out of bed and got ready for the day. She had an appointment out at the Davidson farm to administer shots to two new colts.

As she drove, her mind spun. She couldn't stop thinking about how those objects had ended up at the bottom of the sea. Who put them there? And why those items? Was there something that made them especially compelling? Something that united them? They were all old, but from different periods in England's history. They were all valuable for their historical significance. Were those the unifying factors, or was there more to it?

The visit to the farm was quick, so she found herself with some time before her first appointment at the clinic. She decided to pop in at the church office, but she didn't want to show up unannounced *and* empty-handed, so first she stopped at the Happy Cup Tearoom & Bakery.

She picked out half a dozen iced scones, and then she drove the short distance to White Church, the beautiful old building overlooking the cliffs and the sea far below. She parked in the lot and walked to the side door. Will's car was parked in front of the parsonage, and church secretary Claire Marshall's car was by the door that led to the office.

Harriet grabbed the box of pastries, carried them into the building, and then smiled when she saw Claire at the front desk. She and Claire had become good friends over the previous months.

Claire greeted her warmly. "Hey. I'm afraid Will's in a meeting at the moment."

"That's okay. I'm actually here to see you," Harriet said. "How are you?"

"Oh, I'm fine. The weather is beautiful."

It was cloudy and barely in the sixties, but Harriet wasn't going to argue. Instead, she set the box on Claire's desk. "I come bearing gifts."

"I get the sense you're trying to butter me up for something, and I'll have you know it will absolutely work," Claire said with a grin.

"There's a photo online that's been doctored, and I'm hoping to see if it can be restored to the original," Harriet said. "I wondered if Desmond might be able to help me with that."

Desmond, Claire's thirteen-year-old son, was a computer whiz.

"I'm sure he can, or he'll at least enjoy having a go at it."

"That would be a big help."

"Do you want to send me the picture, or show me where to find it online?"

Harriet showed Claire where she'd found the photo, and Claire promised to send it to Desmond and ask him to take a look.

"Thank you." Harriet's phone rang in her pocket. She pulled it out and saw Dustin's name on the screen.

"That's not a happy face," Claire said. She glanced down at Harriet's phone. "Whoever Dustin is, he must have done something terrible."

"He's my ex-fiancé," Harriet said. "We worked together at a clinic in the States, so when he broke up with me, I just couldn't keep working there. It was one of the reasons I decided to move here last year."

"That would do it," Claire said sympathetically. "Are you going to answer it?"

"Nope." Harriet silenced the ring. "He's coming to the UK and wants to meet up in Yorkshire."

"Are you going to meet him?"

"I don't think so."

"Why not?" Claire cocked her head.

"He says he wants to talk to me, and I don't know that I want to open that wound again. Besides, he's not being particularly respectful of my wishes that he not come."

"It might be good to hear him out," Claire said. "To at least know what he has to say. If he's coming all this way, it must be important."

"That's not why he's coming all the way to England. Apparently, he's going to be in London anyway."

"Surely you're what's bringing him to Yorkshire though. He's not coming up this way to see the sheep."

"We do have some really nice sheep," Harriet said.

"And a lot of them. But that's not what this is about, is it?"

"I guess he's making a trip up here to talk to me."

"So what are you afraid of?" Claire asked.

Her gentle tone drew out the truth. "What if he says he wants to get back together?"

"Then you'll tell him no. You've found someone new, and you've moved on." It sounded so simple when Claire said it like that. "But at least you'd know. Wounds don't heal right if they're still infected, you know."

"Polly agrees with you," Harriet said with a smile. "Something about closure."

Claire smiled too. "Or maybe he doesn't want the relationship again but wants you to come back and work at the clinic with him?"

"I really doubt that."

"But you don't know," Claire said. "I guess that's the point. If you don't hear him out, you'll never know, will you? If you hear what he has to say, it might allow you to move forward more freely. You and I both know that if you don't meet with him, you'll always wonder what he wanted."

Harriet thought about her words for a moment. "That makes sense, but I'm still not convinced."

"Well, think about it. Everyone who loves you will support your decision either way." The phone on Claire's desk began to ring. "And I'll send that picture to Desmond and let you know what he says."

"Thank you." Harriet walked out and got back into her car. She started the engine, and then she listened to the voice mail Dustin had left her.

"Hi, Harriet. I'm leaving for London tonight. Listen, I really need to see you. Can I come up to Yorkshire? Please let me know. I look forward to hearing from you."

Harriet paused before hitting the delete button. Was Claire right? Would it help to hear him out after all?

Before she had a chance to overthink it, she typed a text. MEET ME AT THE CROW'S NEST IN WHITE CHURCH BAY ON SUNDAY AT 1?

His answer came immediately. I'LL SEE YOU THEN!

Harriet put her phone away and put the Beast in gear before she could think too much about what she'd done.

But as she drove, she found that her thoughts weren't centered around Dustin, but those artifacts again. She felt like she was missing something. Why were those three pieces chosen, of all the ancient artifacts that could have been stolen to be smuggled out of the country? Did they share something special?

Or—she couldn't believe she hadn't thought of it before—were there *more* pieces out there? Were there other lobster traps out in the bay with more treasures waiting in them? Had the police checked to see if there were any other traps marked with Miles's buoys? Or had other artifacts already been successfully taken out of the country? She wished there was some way to find out more about the pieces.

But then, of course there was a way. She knew someone who was not only the leading expert on ancient art and artifacts in the region, but also knew Riley better than Harriet did and might be able to give some insight into the young woman and what she might be capable of.

After Harriet parked the Land Rover, she grabbed Dr. Russell's business card and typed out a text to the mobile number listed on it.

HI, DR. RUSSELL, THIS IS HARRIET BAILEY. WE MET YESTERDAY AFTERNOON. I HAVE SOME QUESTIONS ABOUT THE ART THAT WAS DISCOVERED IN THE LOBSTER TRAP, AND I'M TOLD YOU'RE THE EXPERT. WOULD YOU HAVE ANY TIME TO TALK TO ME ABOUT IT?

Her phone buzzed before she even made it all the way to the clinic door. She pulled it back out of her pocket and saw that Dr. Russell had replied.

HI, HARRIET! I ENJOYED TALKING WITH YOU YESTERDAY, AND I WOULD LOVE TO SEE YOU AGAIN. WOULD YOU LIKE TO MEET FOR COFFEE TO DISCUSS?

She typed out, THAT WOULD BE GREAT. WHEN WOULD BE GOOD FOR YOU?

His answer came almost immediately. HOW ABOUT THIS AFTERNOON?

Harriet went through the day in her mind. Will had invited her over for dinner. He was making his famous waffles, which, from what Harriet could tell, were famous because they were one of the few things he knew how to cook.

Still, she didn't need to be at Will's until six, so there was plenty of time after the clinic closed to run over to Whitby for coffee. I COULD DO 4:30.

PERFECT. HOW ABOUT THE THIRSTY GOAT IN THE TOWN CENTER?

The Thirsty Goat? She looked it up and saw that was the name of a coffee shop. SOUNDS GREAT. SEE YOU THEN.

Harriet had to get to work. She slipped her phone back into her pocket and entered the clinic. She took care of two dogs, two kittens, a parakeet, and a potbellied pig before it was time to break for lunch.

When Harriet walked into the waiting room, she found Polly staring through the front window.

"What's going on?" Harriet joined her and saw a police car parked in front of the gallery. Maxwell's little wheels squeaked as he got up from his nap by the counter to follow her across the room.

"They arrived a few minutes ago. I was checking to see if anything exciting was happening."

Poor Maxwell wasn't tall enough to see out the window, so Harriet scooped him up and held him. He pressed his nose against the glass. "I wonder what they want." But Harriet had a guess. The police were probably talking to Riley after what she'd told Van last night. She hoped they were getting something useful out of her—maybe even a confession.

"I don't know." Polly pulled away. "But I guess there's only so long I can stand here before my boss tells me to get back to work."

Harriet laughed. "Your boss is quite the taskmaster." She set Maxwell on the floor, and he trotted to his bed.

"She is, but what can you do?" Polly walked back to her desk and sat down. Charlie, perched on the edge of the desk, swished her tail and offered a plaintive meow. Polly obediently scratched behind the cat's ears.

"I'm going to grab lunch and make a few phone calls," Harriet said. "I'll be here for our next appointment."

As she ate a grilled cheese sandwich and reminded herself yet again that she really needed to get to the store, she reviewed the list of names Mrs. Lewis had given her. Might as well start at the top.

The first name on the list was the chimney sweep. He didn't answer, so she left a voice mail.

The plumber was next on the list. He answered in a gruff voice. "Yeah?"

"Hello? Is this Otto Hughes?"

"Yep. What do you need?"

"I was hoping I might be able to ask you about a job you did in March at Beresford Manor."

"What about it? Something wrong with the work? I can come take another look if something isn't right."

"No, there's nothing wrong with the work that I know of. I'm merely trying to talk to everyone who was visited Beresford Manor in the last couple of months, and your name was on the list."

"Yeah?"

"Can you tell me where you were in the house?" Harriet asked.

"The leak was in the kitchen, so that's where I was. I had to go to the cellar to shut off the water at the main. Creepiest place I've been in a long time. You should see some of the stuff they have down there. But aside from that, I never left the kitchen. Why?"

"Something has gone missing, and we're—"

He interrupted sharply. "You accusing me of stealing something?"

"I'm not accusing you of anything," Harriet replied. "I'm just wondering if you might have seen—"

Otto continued as if she hadn't spoken. "I wouldn't want anything from that old house anyway. It's packed full of spooky old things that no one has wanted in this century. It's probably haunted to boot. Who are you to accuse me anyway?"

"I'm not accusing you of anything," Harriet repeated, trying to keep her voice soothing. "I'm simply asking if you saw anything out of the ordinary."

"Aside from a creepy old house full of creepy old things? No, nothing," he said, and hung up.

Well then.

Harriet moved on to the carpenter—a soft-spoken man with a Scottish lilt, who listened to her questions and explained that he'd had to access both the second and third floors of the house to get to the window with the rotting trim, but he hadn't seen a room full of mysterious objects and hadn't been in that part of the house.

"I do hope you find out what happened to the bust though," he said. "It's terrible to hear something went missing. These old homes are filled with so many historical treasures. I'd love to poke around and explore some of them someday."

It was hard to tell over the phone, but he sounded genuine enough that Harriet was inclined to believe him. She'd do some more research on him, though, to be on the safe side. She left a message for the exterminator and then called the number she found on the website of the Heritage Commission and left a voice mail, asking to speak to David.

It was almost time to get back to work, but just as she started to get up to wash her plate, Polly called.

"Hi," Harriet said into her phone.

"Sorry to bother you, but the police are here, and they want to talk to you."

"I'll be right over."

CHAPTER FIFTEEN

Harriet walked through the door that led to the clinic and found Sergeant Oduba and DI McCormick seated in the waiting room. Van spoke quietly with Polly, their heads close together.

"Good afternoon, Harriet." DI McCormick gave her a tight smile.

"Hello, Sergeant Oduba. DI McCormick." Harriet gestured. "Maybe we should step into my office. We'll have patients arriving shortly."

The officers followed her down the hallway and sat in the chairs across from her desk. Van brought in an additional chair for himself. Harriet sat behind the desk and waited for them to tell her what was going on.

"Van tells us you spoke with him last night, and we wanted to ask you a bit more about a few things that came up," DI McCormick said.

"Sure." Harriet saw that Van's face was set, betraying nothing. "What do you need?"

"First off, let's talk about what your receptionist told Officer Worthington about the email address used to contact Liam Beresford. You are saying it was not Mason McGinnis's. Can you tell us how you came to that conclusion?" Sergeant Oduba asked.

"Mason told us," Harriet said. "Polly and I went to York and talked to him."

"When did you speak with Mr. McGinnis?" DI McCormick asked.

"Wednesday," Harriet said. "Polly and I stopped by his shop. It's full of beautiful old antiques. Mason was incredibly nice, and when we were chatting with him, we mentioned the Roman bust he'd tried to buy from Liam Beresford. He had no idea what we were talking about, which was our first indication something was wrong. Then we showed him a copy of the email sent to Liam, and he pointed out that it wasn't his email address. Someone created a fake email account using his name."

"Let's go back a bit," DI McCormick said. "You said you 'stopped by' his shop. The shop is in York. How did you and Ms. Thatcher happen to be in York?"

For a moment Harriet considered whether to pretend they'd had a strong hankering for antiques, but then decided better of it. "We went there to speak with Mason. I'm sorry if we overstepped. We didn't mean to. But I talked to Liam Beresford—"

"How did you happen to speak to Lord Beresford?" Sergeant Oduba asked. "We've had a hard time getting in to see him."

"Liam and I have been friendly since last summer when he went missing and I helped locate him," Harriet said. "So I stopped by to talk to him."

"Can you tell us the content of your conversation with Lord Beresford?" Sergeant Oduba asked.

Harriet had the feeling she was being grilled, and she did her best to keep a cool head. "I asked him about the bust, and he told me about the email he got from Mason McGinnis—well, from someone pretending to be Mason McGinnis. He also told me he got an email from Riley Sloane, a student who wanted to write a paper about the piece. He didn't respond to either email, and he didn't realize the bust was gone until you showed up asking about it on Tuesday."

"How would he not notice the absence of such a valuable piece?" DI McCormick asked.

"He showed me the room where the bust was, and it's actually not that hard to see how he might not have noticed," Harriet told them. "It was packed to the brim with stuff. Mrs. Lewis gave me printouts of the emails he received about it. That's what I showed to Mason, and, like I said, he pointed out that the email address was wrong."

Sergeant Oduba cleared his throat. "You also told DC Worthington that the fake email address was also connected with the bowl that was found in the trap. Can you tell us more about that?"

"Sure."

She told them about her visit to Matilda's father's cottage and about Matilda's sale of the bowl. Then she answered questions about her conversations with Oscar Ramirez and Johnny Bradley. Given the looks on their faces, she expected to be chastised for becoming too involved in the investigation, but what she felt in their questions was actually a grudging respect.

"How did you happen to make the connection between Riley Sloane, who is studying ancient art, and Johnny Bradley, who knows about lobsters?" DI McCormick asked.

"If you mean how we found out they knew each other, that was easy," Harriet said. "We met Johnny in the parking lot when he picked Riley up after her shift the other night. She introduced him as her boyfriend. Polly found Johnny on social media within minutes, saw that he worked at the marine research center at the university, and made the connection."

They didn't ask her about her visit to see Johnny at the research center, and Harriet wasn't sure whether to bring it up. But while she considered it, DI McCormick asked a question she wasn't expecting.

"What can you tell us about Whitby Whale Watch Tours?"

It took a moment for Harriet to get past her surprise and find her voice again. "Nothing. I've been whale watching back in the States, but I've never done it here. I know tours leave from the marina, but I've never given them any thought. Why?"

"You haven't spoken to anyone about a recent tour?"

"No." Though now she wished she had. "Why?"

Instead of answering, the police officers looked at one another, and then, as if there was some unspoken signal, they all stood.

"Thank you for speaking with us," Sergeant Oduba said. Harriet waited for him to demand that she stay out of the investigation, but he didn't. "If you learn anything more, will you continue to let us know?"

"Of course." Harriet waited for them to file out so she could move toward the door, but when the other two officers went out into the hallway, Van hung back.

"Sorry about that," he said. "They had to follow up on your tips officially."

"I don't mean to be in the way or interfere with the investigation," Harriet said. "I just promised Myles Stafford I would help discover who took out the permit in his name."

"I know that, and they know that. Your and Polly's tip about the fake email account was good. Oduba had the tech guys look into it, and they found something very interesting. Something that makes your friend Johnny even more worth looking into."

"What?" Harriet asked.

"The emails all came from the same IP address, and it's a computer on the University of Whitby network. That's important, because in order for any electronic device to have access to the university's network, it has to be registered. We're working with their IT team to figure out exactly which computer it was and who it's registered to."

Harriet was pretty sure she understood this. An IP—internet protocol—address was like a physical address, and each computer had one. It shouldn't take them long to trace the address to that particular computer. "With any luck, it'll be someone's laptop and not a more public computer in the library or computer lab," she said.

"Bingo. It was a good tip." Van grinned at her then turned and left, walking quickly to catch up with the other police officers.

Harriet was left to puzzle over what he'd told her. The fake McGinnis emails had been sent from someone using the university's network. Johnny lived on campus, solidifying his position as her prime suspect.

She also wanted nothing more than to figure out why the police had asked her about a whale watching tour. But for now, it was time to get back to work.

CHAPTER SIXTEEN

Harriet was distracted by the case for the rest of the afternoon, though she tried to focus on her work. By the time her last patient was led out the door on a sparkly rhinestone leash, she was itching to get going.

"I'll clean up," Polly said. "I have to wait for Angus to pick me up anyway."

"Are you sure?" Harriet hated to keep leaving such tasks to Polly. They were supposed to be a team after all.

"I'll be here anyway, so I might as well make myself useful," Polly said. "Go have fun."

Harriet wasn't sure *fun* was the right term, but she thanked Polly and drove to Whitby, reflecting that she was putting plenty of miles on the Beast this week. Or, rather, plenty of kilometers.

The town center of Whitby was a cluster of historic buildings clinging to the hillsides that surrounded the harbor. The Thirsty Goat was a quaint shop with exposed beams and worn wooden floors and warm salmon-colored walls. The building was clearly very old, and a plaque on the wall explained that parts of it dated to the seventeenth century. She found Dr. Russell sitting on a bench just inside the door, his nose in a paperback mystery.

"Harriet." He smiled, and the skin at the corners of his eyes crinkled. He stood and tucked the book into the pocket of his canvas jacket. He wore a button-down with jeans and trendy black sneakers. The brand name on the side seemed French, but she had never heard of it. "It's good to see you again."

"Dr. Russell. It's good to see you too. Thank you for meeting me."

"Please, call me Jackson. I'm really glad you reached out. Shall we?" He led her to the counter, where he ordered a double espresso. "Just don't tell anyone I ordered coffee instead of tea, okay? They might revoke my British passport if anyone found out."

"Your secret is safe with me," Harriet said, and ordered a latte for herself.

He pulled out his wallet to pay.

"This should be on me, since I reached out to you," Harriet protested.

"I'm already drinking coffee instead of tea," he replied with a grin, handing a card to the cashier. "I don't need to risk my good standing as a gentleman in the same day."

"I'm sorry, do you have another card?" the cashier asked after a moment.

Jackson narrowed his eyes. "That one's been finicky recently. The stripe on the back is wearing off, and I keep meaning to order a new one. Here, use this one instead." He handed over a different credit card, which went through with no problem.

They settled at a table in the corner, near bookshelves stuffed with books and board games and magazines of all kinds.

"So," he said, gazing at her over the rim of his tiny cup. "What did you want to know about that art?"

"I'm trying to figure out why those particular pieces were taken," Harriet said. "I mean, of all the pieces in the museum, and with all the important artifacts kept in attics all over Yorkshire, why were those three pieces chosen? What ties them together, or what makes them special?"

"Because they're the best of the best," he said without hesitation. "If you're looking for a textbook example of art from the Roman-era settlements, that bust of Marcus Aurelius can't be beat. It's gorgeous, and so significant."

He grew more animated as he continued. "And the Neolithic period—it always blows my mind to think that we're talking about thousands and thousands of years ago. A whole bowl, fully intact and so astonishingly well-preserved? It's an archaeologist's dream. My colleague Bettler is jealous that I got to see it. He's never found anything so complete in all his excavations."

And it had been hiding in a private collection for decades. Not for the first time, Harriet wondered how many other treasures still were.

"And the coins?" He shook his head. "Artifacts from the Norse settlements might be the rarest of them all. I know they probably don't look like much, but those coins could be the most valuable and rare pieces in the country. Did you know York was the capital of the Viking settlements in the UK?"

"I had no idea," Harriet replied.

"It was called Jorvik, which is where we get the name York. There's a great museum there about the different periods in English history. You should check it out. I served on the advisory board for the Norse part of the display, and I wrote a book about Jorvik a few years back. It was such a fascinating time in our British history. Come to my office later, and I'll give you a copy."

"Thank you. That would be great." She took a sip of her latte. "So what you're saying is, the thief has good taste."

"Impeccable. I couldn't believe it when I saw what was in those containers. I feel lucky to have been allowed to be there. The thief was certainly someone who knew what they were doing. Though, honestly, I wish they'd shown a bit more breadth. Why is there nothing from the Anglo-Saxon period? If you want a full tour of the history of the people who've called this land home, you have to include them. And nothing from the Normans? Feels like an oversight to me. When they find the thief, I have some questions."

"I've been wondering if there were more pieces from different time periods that haven't been found yet," Harriet said. "Maybe they were already taken out of the country or were about to be taken out to drop into lobster traps when these were discovered."

His eyes widened. "That's an intriguing possibility. I'd feel much better about the whole thing if you were to tell me that the Anglo-Saxon and Norman periods were represented after all. I mean, obviously I wouldn't *want* more art stolen, but at least I would know that the thief didn't skip over those periods."

Harriet laughed despite herself. "Then you think it would need to be a professional of some kind? Someone who knows the art or archaeology world well?"

"Or someone who has good connections." He gave her a smile that many women probably found charming. Women who weren't dating

Will Knight, anyway. "I just thank God those pieces were recovered before they were lost forever. When I think how close they came…" He pressed his lips together then said, "I sure hope they find whoever did this. Putting priceless artifacts into salt water at the bottom of the sea could have been disastrous. And in a lobster trap, of all things."

"What do you mean?"

"It seems so odd, doesn't it? A lobster trap?" He shrugged. "Maybe it's just that lobsters freak me out, with their creepy antennae and their big claws."

"They taste good though."

"I've never been a fan. There's a reason they're called the cockroaches of the sea."

She grinned then returned to the subject at hand. "So, is the only connection between the artifacts that they're the best examples of their kind? There's nothing more to it than that?"

He cocked his head. "What kind of connection are you looking for?"

She thought for a moment. "I don't know. I guess I was hoping you might be able to tell me. I thought maybe there's some obvious connection between the artifacts that would explain why they were chosen, and I thought you could point me to some ideas about who stole them. Which I guess is kind of silly, now that I'm saying it out loud."

"Not silly at all." He leaned forward. "That's an interesting angle. Maybe we just need to think about it differently. As in, where were the artifacts going? Perhaps you're too concerned with making connections on this end when the question that really needs answering is, what was their original destination? Maybe that would tell you something about how they got there."

"I guess what makes the most sense is that they would end up in someone's private collection," Harriet said.

"That's a good guess." Jackson nodded. "Most stolen art does, you know. Then it's either held by the collectors or sold again on the black market."

"I guess I shouldn't be surprised that there's a black market for ancient art."

"I think there's a black market for everything," he said. "I've heard rumors about a handful of Russian oligarchs who have a taste for early Anglo-Saxon artwork, though these are obviously not from that period. But maybe you'd have more luck if you started there."

"Where would I even start to find out which Russian oligarchs collect stolen artwork from the black market?" Harriet asked.

"Well, now that you say it like that, I see the problem," he said. "I suppose even if you could, you probably wouldn't want to. They don't seem like the kind of people most of us would want to get tangled up with."

Harriet sighed. That line of questioning wasn't getting her anywhere. If there really wasn't more of a connection than the fact that the pieces were all excellent examples of their period, then there wasn't much more he could tell her.

But she did have another question for him. "You must be a very busy man, teaching and writing books. How many students do you advise on top of that?"

"Only a handful per year. My department isn't all that big, but we're lucky because we get some of the most gifted students in the university, if you ask me."

"How long have you been working with Riley Sloane?"

"For a couple of years now. She's one of the bright stars in our department. I expect her to go far if she keeps at it."

"How well do you know her?"

"We mostly discuss projects she's working on or papers she's writing, but we do talk about other subjects sometimes. I know she lives at home with her parents and they don't understand why she's studying 'old junk.' I get the sense they would prefer she study business or premed or prelaw or something similar."

"I read the paper she wrote about the Roman bust."

"Yes, she found an old newspaper article from back when the bust was acquired—in the 1940s, I believe—and used that as her main source. I was impressed. I didn't even know the piece existed until she wrote about it, and this is what I do for a living. That's what I mean about her going far. She's got creativity as well as brains, and that counts for a lot in this field."

Harriet thought carefully about how to phrase her next question, knowing it could easily come off the wrong way. "Do you think there's any way that creativity could lead her to push the limits a bit too much?"

"What do you mean?" He cocked his head.

"I mean that she's one of the few people with knowledge of the bust and the Neolithic period, and clearly she has a good advisor. I guess I'm wondering if maybe, well—"

"No." He said it emphatically but then said, "At least, I don't think so."

Harriet waited, letting him mull it over.

At last he said, "I mean, I see what you're getting at, I suppose. Do I think she had anything to do with it? No, I can't really see that.

But I see why you're asking. She has the knowledge to recognize a good piece when she sees it, and there aren't many who do." Suddenly, Jackson's eyes popped wide. "Oh wow. Her boyfriend, Johnny. He works at the marine research center, doesn't he?"

Harriet nodded, glad she didn't have to spell it out. "He works with the lobsters."

He tossed back the rest of his espresso and set the cup down. "I would have said there was no way. I mean, she's such a good kid. I never would have believed that she might be behind something like that, but that's a pretty hard link to ignore. I can't believe I didn't see it before." He adjusted the espresso cup on the saucer. "I've always thought I was a pretty good judge of character, but maybe…" His voice trailed off.

"It's nothing more than a theory," Harriet said. "Obviously it's not one anyone wants to be true."

"See? That's what I mean. I'm usually a good judge of character. I could tell right away that you're a kind, generous person who wants to see the best in everyone. I could also tell that you're smart, and funny, and someone who would be interesting to talk to. And I was right about that too."

Was he flirting? "Now you're being ridiculous."

He grinned. "I don't think so, but I don't really know enough about you to be sure. So tell me more about yourself, Harriet Bailey. You're from the States, right?"

"Connecticut."

"And you're a veterinarian?"

"Yes. I came to take over my grandfather's practice when he died."

"I'm sorry to hear that. About your grandfather, not that you came here. I'm quite glad that you came here, in fact."

She took a sip of her drink. As flattered as she was by the attention, she wasn't interested in encouraging it. She intentionally kept any flirtation out of her tone. "And you? If we're judging by accents, you're not from Yorkshire originally, are you?"

"Guilty as charged. I grew up in London and went to Oxford. After I got my PhD, Whitby offered me a place, so here I am."

"And how did you end up studying archaeology?"

"My original plan was to sail around the world and be a pirate, but that didn't work out as well as I'd hoped."

"It's hard to make a living as a pirate these days," Harriet said. "Plus, peg legs aren't as readily available as you'd think."

"Exactly. So I settled for archaeology instead. But Vikings have been an excellent consolation prize."

"Vikings were basically a society of pirates, weren't they?"

"Exactly! I tried to do medicine like my parents wanted—they're like Riley's in that way—but I couldn't stop dreaming about unearthing secrets from the past hidden right below our feet. My parents weren't thrilled, but it was their own fault. They're the ones who took me to Egypt, Greece, and Rome and showed me the remains of ancient civilizations. How could I not fall in love with the past?"

"It is fascinating," Harriet said. "Why didn't your parents want you to study archaeology?"

"Not prestigious enough," he said. "They don't understand why I like digging around in the dirt."

"You're a university professor. That's not prestigious enough?"

"I don't know. I suppose maybe it's more that it doesn't bring in a fat paycheck."

They talked for a while longer about his upbringing—which involved plenty of sailboats, vacations to far-flung destinations, and mild neglect from his high-society parents—and his research and the two children he had with his ex-wife, and soon it was time for Harriet to get going.

"Hang on, come back to my office so I can grab that book for you," he said.

Harriet glanced at her watch. She didn't have much time left to get to dinner at Will's. "It'll have to be fast. I'm meeting my boy-friend for dinner."

"The office is only a few blocks from here. I promise to let you go in plenty of time to meet the luckiest man in England."

He was a shameless flirt. She wondered how often it worked for him. She got the sense he was used to women responding well, which didn't endear him to her—and increased her appreciation for Will.

But she had to admit she was curious about his office, and he really seemed to want to get her a copy of his book, so she followed him out of the coffee shop and down the few blocks to the leafy campus.

They went inside the same building she'd been in before, where the archaeology department was, and up a set of creaky wooden stairs to his office. Sunlight flooded in through the mullioned win-dows, and the walls were lined with bookshelves stuffed with leather spines. A large wooden desk took up most of the space, while a small sitting area with an overstuffed couch and chairs sat against the far wall. Copies of his degrees hung on the walls, and framed pictures stood on his desk and on the edges of the bookshelves.

"This is beautiful." Harriet stepped forward to examine a picture of a much-younger Jackson on the bow of a boat. It appeared to be in some tropical location, judging by the turquoise color of the water and the palm trees.

"That was my grandfather's boat. He loved to sail all over the world."

"Was *he* a pirate?"

"Sadly, no. Just a man with too much money who loved to spoil his grandson."

"That doesn't sound so bad."

"It was the best." Jackson walked over to a bookshelf and ran his fingertip over the spines of the books, searching for the right one.

Harriet moved on to look at several of the other photos, including one with a high-school-aged Jackson in a school uniform, his arms around several friends, a beautiful old building in the background. There was also a photo that showed him and what must have been his two young daughters in front of the Eiffel Tower and one of him on some sort of archaeological dig, dressed in khaki pants and a sand-colored shirt. If he was trying to project the image of a wealthy, well-traveled, learned professor, he had nailed it.

"Here you go," he said, holding out a thick hardcover. *The History and Culture of the Norse Settlements in the UK.* "Now if you have trouble sleeping, you have a solution." Despite his self-deprecation, he was clearly proud of it.

"Thank you. I look forward to reading it."

"Let me know if you have any more questions," he said. "I'd love to see you again and help however I can."

"Will do."

She carried the book down the stairs and hurried back to the Land Rover. She mulled over the encounter as she drove. As much as she was excited for an evening with Will, she knew she needed to tell him that she planned to meet up with Dustin on Sunday, and she wasn't sure how he would react.

She said a prayer, asking for the Lord's help and guidance. She was going to need it.

CHAPTER SEVENTEEN

The parsonage of White Church was a lovely stone cottage with a steeply sloped roof and a thriving garden. It was cozy and charming, but whenever Harriet thought about her and Will together as husband and wife, she liked to imagine them at her house—waking up beside him, enjoying long leisurely breakfasts together, and snuggling on the couch at night.

She hoped someday it would come true, but she trusted that God would make His will for her clear with continued prayer. She wasn't about to make a mistake like she had with Dustin and jump in without knowing God was at the center of everything she and Will did as a couple. Some days, she truly hoped it would happen. Other days, she wasn't sure she trusted in second chances, didn't know if she could believe that things would be different this time.

Will answered the door with a big smile and ushered her inside with a kiss. The windows were open, and the cottage felt warm and welcoming.

"It smells great in here," Harriet said. "Are you making bacon?"

"You have to have bacon with waffles," Will said. "It's the law. Isn't that the way it is in the US?"

"It should be," Harriet said. The aroma of the bacon and the maple syrup heating on the stove drew her into the kitchen. Ash

Wednesday, Will's gray kitten, meowed a welcome from his perch on the edge of the table.

"Hello, Ash." Harriet went over and patted his head.

"He's not really supposed to sit on the table," Will said.

"Does he know that?" Ash purred and stretched his neck up as she stroked his fur.

"He knows it well enough. He just doesn't care."

"Sounds like a cat to me."

She asked Will about his day, and as he cooked the waffles, he talked to her about the new-members class he was leading and a pipe that had burst at the church. Then he asked her about her day.

"It was kind of odd," she said. "It started with a visit to the church this morning and then went downhill from there."

"You came to the church and didn't say hi?"

"Claire said you were in a meeting," Harriet said. "I didn't want to interrupt."

"You're more interesting than a budget meeting any day."

"That's a really low bar."

Will laughed. "What did you need?"

"I needed a young person." Harriet explained why she asked Claire for Desmond's help with the social media photo and then went over all the evidence that made Johnny and Riley seem the most likely suspects.

"So she knows about art, and he was out on the water pulling up lobster traps, possibly with the right-color buoys, the day before the art was discovered," Will said.

"And he lives on campus, which is where the fake emails were sent from. And he's short on money. He showed me some photos on his phone, and his roommate happened to send him some telling text messages at the time," Harriet said.

"Which could be because he didn't get the payout he counted on." Will shooed Ash off the table and then set plates of waffles down at their places. They said grace, and he continued. "He and Riley sound like a suspicious pair. Who else could it be? Where are you on the other suspects?"

"What do you mean who else? It has to be Johnny and Riley," she said. "Who else is there?"

"You had a whole list of suspects the other day," Will said. "What happened to them? Have you eliminated them?"

"No, but Johnny and Riley..." She let her voice trail off, realizing he was right. "I mean, I guess I sort of just assumed no one else was guilty once I found out about those two."

"But shouldn't we look at all sides? Not jump to conclusions?" Will asked. "You said Johnny denied any involvement. What happens if we assume he's telling the truth?"

Harriet gave him a fake scowl. "You know, you have this really annoying habit of seeing the best in people and asking fair questions."

"It's a character flaw, I know. Hazard of the job." He drizzled syrup over his waffle. "So?"

"Fine," Harriet said grudgingly. "Mason McGinnis is the antiques dealer we thought sent emails about those pieces, but we know it was a fake email address set up in his name, so it wasn't him."

"Unless he set up the fake email account himself," Will said. "If it even is fake, as he claimed."

"I thought we were believing what people say," Harriet teased. "But why would he do that? Why draw attention to himself with an identifiable email address and then steal one of the pieces he asked about? Besides, he doesn't have access to the university network, so that doesn't sound plausible."

"Fair enough. What about Shane O'Grady?"

"Shane insists that he's turned over a new leaf. He denies having anything to do with it. But he's also got a demonstrated track record of breaking the law when it comes to shellfish."

"And shellfish law is very strict, as we all know," Will said.

She shook her head. "I don't think he's eliminated entirely, but we haven't been able to establish any connection between him and anyone who knows about art. Additionally, his previous missteps strike me as rather impulsive and poorly thought out, so I don't see him masterminding something like this. And Martina at the marina—"

Will chuckled. "Martina at the marina? She's in the right business, isn't she?"

"I didn't even think of that," Harriet said with a smile. "She's sure he wasn't the one who registered for the permit in Myles's name."

"Has she seen photos of the other suspects?"

"No. That's a good idea though. I could show her pictures and see if she recognizes any of them."

"In the meantime, I'd like to believe Shane O'Grady really has started fresh. Which leaves us with…?"

"I'm trying to find out about the volunteers at the Atkinson Museum. The guard on duty thought one of them might have been involved with the theft. But then again, the guard was the one who was blamed, so maybe we should take that with a grain of salt. Although he didn't appear to understand why the coins that were taken were so valuable."

"What have you found out about the volunteers?"

"That the museum doesn't list their names on its site. In other words, not very much," she admitted. "I have a list of people who were in Liam Beresford's house during the time period the bust was taken. It's a short list."

"He doesn't entertain a lot."

"So far, I've talked to a carpenter I don't think was involved and a plumber who was surly and didn't tell me much. I'm waiting for a couple others to call me back. One of them is likely the person who stole the bust, and hopefully there's a connection between that person and the one who posed as Mason McGinnis and bought the Neolithic bowl from Matilda."

"Was one of them Johnny or Riley?"

"Not as far as I know."

"So Riley may have had knowledge of the bust but not necessarily the access."

"But she could have paid someone to steal it. Maybe she's friends with the plumber. I don't know."

"Maybe." But he didn't sound convinced. "Are either of them friends with any of the volunteers at the Atkinson Museum? Or the guard?"

"I don't know. One or both of them could have known about the lax security through any of the volunteers, I guess."

"It seems like there are still a lot of questions about how Johnny and Riley could have managed it all."

"Or how anyone could have, really." Harriet took a bite and thought for a moment. Will's waffles really were very good—light and fluffy, with just the right amount of sweetness.

"So what are we missing?" Will asked.

"I don't know. Part of me still wonders, why these pieces in particular? Or were there more, and only a few were discovered? Could there be a whole museum's worth of treasures in lobster traps all over the North Sea?"

"That's a disturbing thought," Will said.

"Or is there something about the stolen pieces that could tell us who did it?"

"Maybe," Will said. "Or maybe it was simply proximity."

"What do you mean?"

"I mean maybe the thief grabbed what he could. Maybe he reached out to dozens of people who have antiquities in their attics and cased museums all over the countryside but ended up stealing only the things he could get. Or buying them outright, for a fraction of what they were worth. But maybe the sole unifying factor is that these are the items the thief was able to get his hands on."

It made so much sense when Will said it that she couldn't believe she hadn't seen it herself. "You might be right. I could be driving myself crazy trying to find a connection where none exists."

"Or maybe Riley is the connection," he said, dunking a piece of bacon in his syrup. "Since she's been on a Neolithic dig and was the one who knew about the bust being in Lord Beresford's private collection. Maybe it really was her."

"So now you're saying I'm right and it is her?"

"No, I'm saying let's not miss something because we're convinced we know what happened. Let's make sure not to ignore facts that don't line up with our preferred theory."

"That's annoyingly good advice."

"I try." Will grinned at her. Jackson Russell may have the whole charming, self-deprecating professor thing down pat, but she would take Will any day.

She picked up a piece of bacon, dripping with syrup, and took a bite. She thought back through her day, searching for any facts she'd overlooked because they didn't fit her chosen narrative.

"The police did say one strange thing when they were questioning me today," Harriet said.

"Wait, what?" Will dropped his fork onto his plate with a clatter. "The police questioned you?"

"Not the way you're thinking," Harriet said. "I mean, they were asking me about what I knew and all that, but I'm not a suspect or anything. I called Van with some tips last night, and his superiors needed to follow up on that. They also asked if I'd talked to anyone who'd been on a whale-watching tour recently out of Whitby."

"I did a tour a few years back. It leaves from the harbor, and they take you out where the whales live, and if you're lucky, you'll see some. We saw some humpbacks breaching and slapping the water with their fins. It was amazing. But why were they asking you about it?"

"I don't know," Harriet said. "I suppose there must be a connection to the case somehow."

"Let's see what we can find out." Will pushed his plate aside, retrieved his laptop, and sat down in the chair beside hers. He opened the laptop and pulled up the website for Whitby Whale Watch Tours. The webpage showed a whale breaching out of the sea against a sunset sky. Will clicked on different tabs, and together they searched for any hint of what might have been the clue the police were fishing around about. *Tag your photos with #Whitby WhaleWatchTours* read the line at the top of each page.

"I don't know," Will said. "I don't see anything. Did you ask Van?"

"There wasn't an opportunity at the time," Harriet said. "And I don't want to call him now and interrupt his date with Polly." She grinned at Will. "Maybe you should do it. He can't say no to his minister."

Will laughed and grabbed his phone from the counter. "Why not?" He put the phone on speaker and set it on the table between them. It rang and rang but went to voice mail.

Harriet pulled out her own phone and tried him, but her call also went to voice mail. "At least we know it's not personal. They're probably at the theater. I'll see if I can get him tomorrow."

"You'll have to tell me what he says." Will started gathering the empty plates.

"I will." She took a deep breath. If she was going to bring up the topic of Dustin, she needed to do it soon. She mustered her courage, and then she said, "Actually—"

"Harriet—" Will said at the same moment. He stopped and patted his pocket. "Sorry, you go ahead."

"Okay. Thanks. There's actually something I wanted to talk to you about."

"What's that?" Will's smile faded. "Why do I get the sense it isn't good?"

"It's fine, I promise. It's just that—" She was making a mess of this already. "Dustin texted me."

"Your ex?"

"He's in the UK, and he asked if I could meet up with him. He wants to talk."

"I see."

Harriet's inability to read his tone made her nervous, which made her start to babble. "At first I said no, because I don't want to see him. But he kept pushing, saying he really needed to talk to me. Now he's traveled all the way here and is coming to Yorkshire on Sunday, and I said I would meet him at the Crow's Nest to talk to him. I'm sure it's nothing, and I promise you there's nothing between us anymore, which is why I didn't want to see him. But the more I thought about it and the more people I talked to—well, it seemed like maybe I should hear what he had to say. But I won't go if you're not comfortable with it."

Will was quiet, his expression solemn. Finally, he said, "You're absolutely right. You should hear him out."

Whatever she'd expected him to say, it hadn't been that. "You really think so?"

"I do. I can't pretend I'm thrilled about you meeting up with the man you thought you'd be spending the rest of your life with, but you need to hear what he has to say."

Harriet nodded. "You have nothing to worry about, Will. What Dustin and I had is long over, and it's for the best that it ended. It's you I care about. But thank you for understanding."

"I'll be waiting to hear how it goes. Anxiously."

All of a sudden, Harriet wished she could take it back. She would do anything to avoid hurting Will, and she could tell he was upset about what might happen.

But he was, as always, gracious and kind. "I love you, Harriet, and I trust you."

Harriet would do anything in the world not to violate that trust. After a moment's silence, she asked, "What was it you were going to say?"

"Oh, nothing," Will said. "It can wait."

As she drove home that night, Harriet thanked God for Will—for sweet, gentle, kind, trusting Will, and she prayed that God would bless him and guide her conversation with Dustin.

After she'd taken Maxwell out and taken a shower, Harriet was still wound up. It had been a long, full day, and she should be tired, but mostly she was itchy with the sense that she was missing something obvious. In her conversations with Will, with Jackson Russell, with the police, she couldn't shake the sense that there was something there, just out of reach.

She sat down at her laptop, uncertain what she was going to do. She opened it, and then, for lack of any better ideas, ran a search for *art lobster traps Whitby*.

The first thing that came up was the article in the most recent *Whitby Gazette*. She clicked on it and reread the story she'd seen in the paper earlier, hunting for clues that might tell her something new. But it was the same piece. She read to the bottom, and then let her eyes drift down to the comments section.

What a waste of police manpower and money! Who cares about some old rusty metal? Let's get the police to focus on out-of-control crime.

If something suspicious happens at the marina, there's exactly one person who is responsible. Hopefully the police will be smart enough to talk to Shady O'Grady.

I couldn't get a lobster permit this year, and now they're giving them to criminals? The incompetence is astounding.

There were several more comments in this same vein, and she was about to power off the computer and go read a book to try to calm her mind, when something caught her eye. She read it quickly, and then, leaning forward, reread it more slowly.

The comment came from someone who said they'd been on a whale-watching tour on Saturday, and—well, it was very interesting.

CHAPTER EIGHTEEN

Someone on a Whitby Whale Watch tour saw the guy pulling up the trap on Saturday," Harriet blurted when Will answered her call. "That's why the police were asking about the whale-watching tour. Someone on that boat saw it happen."

"What?"

"I found it in the comments section in the online newspaper article."

Will seemed to take her revelation in stride. "Making this the first time in history something useful was said in the comments."

"Here's what Babsgreeley5634 said: 'I think I saw the guy do it. I can't believe it. I was on the whale-watching tour, and we passed by an area where there were a lot of buoys. There was a guy pulling up a trap. It had to be the criminal, because I saw him put a box of some kind into the trap. My husband, Wayne, saw it too. I forgot all about it until just now, but I'm sure I saw him. The whales were cool, but they didn't hold still long enough to take good pictures. They're kind of like my grandchildren that way.'"

"Wow. There's a lot to unpack there. First off, Babs was upset because the whales didn't pose for her?"

Harriet laughed. "Apparently."

She could hear his warm smile. "Right. So this is probably what the police were referring to."

"I imagine so. But how far out in the ocean was this lobster trap? How were there whales near it? How did she see the guy from a whale-watching tour?"

"The whales are much farther out than lobster traps would typically be," Will said. "Sometimes they come in closer, but in general they live way out in the deep water, far from shore, so that's where the whale-watching boats head."

"And there are no lobsters out there?"

"There might be, but good luck getting a rope long enough to lower your trap down to the bottom of the ocean. The lobster gatherers tend to stay in the shallower water, closer to shore."

"So how would this woman have seen someone pulling up a lobster trap from a whale-watching boat?"

"She must have seen him as they were traveling through the shallow water to get to deep water."

"Ah. That makes sense." Harriet felt a little silly for asking the question. "So we should find Babsgreeley 5634."

"How many Barbara Greeleys can there be?"

Harriet already had a search window open. "Here's a social media page for one in Scarborough."

"That sounds likely. I'm looking her up too." She heard Will typing on his end of the line.

Harriet clicked on Barbara's page and started poking around. "She mostly posts pictures of her grandchildren or what she made for dinner. Oh, but here's mention of a man named Wayne."

"I bet that's her."

"I'm sending a message to Barbara now."

"I knew you'd figure it out," Will said.

"Well, let's see what Barbara has to say. It may be another dead end."

Will stayed positive. "Or she could have the answer to this whole thing."

Harriet was still keyed up after she got off the phone with Will. She needed something to settle her mind.

She looked around and spotted the book Jackson Russell had given her earlier. He did say it would help if she couldn't sleep. She took it to bed with her and opened it.

The History and Culture of the Norse Settlements in the UK
By Dr. Jackson Russell
Introduction

In this book, I will chronicle the rise and fall of the Norse, or Scandinavian, rule of the lands we now call the United Kingdom. In particular, I will focus on the historical record left behind in the earth, slowly being excavated and studied, that tells us more about the Norse settlements in the Yorkshire area. I will also discuss what they tell us about how these ancient civilizations lived and worked.

The Norse arrived in the area around 865 CE and invaded, conquering the land that had been claimed by the Anglo-Saxon people since the Romans withdrew around

400 CE. The army, led by Ivar the Boneless and his brother Halfdan Ragnarsson, made its way north to Northumbria where the Anglo-Saxons were embroiled in a civil war. In 862 the ruler of Northumbria, Oshbert, was deposed by Ælla of Northumbria. Ivar the Boneless was able to capitalize on the Anglo-Saxons' disarray and captured York in 866/ 867....

Harriet slept deeply Friday night, soothed to sleep by the convoluted academic prose in Jackson Russell's book. Even encountering names like Ivar the Boneless couldn't make the book interesting, though she did find one section while she was skimming that indicated the Norse settlements had minted coins in the area.

The discussion about the coins was as opaque as the rest of the writing, but she took it to mean that Jackson was right about the importance of coins from the Viking period. There was even a picture of the ones that had been on display in the Atkinson Museum, and in the text, Jackson described advising the curators at the museum.

Harriet got up when Charlie started meowing at her door. She reluctantly rolled over and climbed out of bed, and after she'd cared for both animals, she started the coffee, bleary-eyed.

It was a beautiful, sunny Saturday morning, with a hint of chill in the air. For a moment, Harriet had visions of a nice walk along the cliffs and a long lazy afternoon reading, but then reality set in. The clinic was open until noon, and after that she had to finally make it to the grocery store. On top of that, there were other avenues to investigate, and—

But first, coffee. Once she had a full cup and a bowl of oatmeal, Harriet sat down at the table with her Bible and a journal. She read more about Paul's metamorphosis and everything he suffered, all in the name of spreading the good news. Paul, who had been the worst persecutor of Christians, had truly changed. No one, and no circumstance, was outside the power of God's transformation. She sent up a prayer of gratitude for such guidance in her own life.

Then she pushed herself to her feet, cleaned the kitchen, swept the floor, and tossed in a load of laundry.

That done, she checked her social media messages. Aha! She had a message back from Barbara Greeley.

Hello. Yes, I saw the thief putting that art into the trap, and I'm happy to tell you about it. I'm free today outside of picking up my heart medication.

Barbara gave a phone number. Harriet saw that she had sent the message twenty minutes before, so she was awake. She picked up her phone and punched in the numbers.

"Hello?"

"Hello, this is Harriet Bailey. I sent you a message about—"

"Yeah, the whale-watching tour. I've never done whale-watching before, but it was Maya's birthday, so she wanted us all to go. At first I said there was no way I was paying those prices when I could watch whales on TV at home, but then she offered to pay for my ticket, so how could I say no?"

"That was nice of her." It seemed like the right thing to say. "Can you tell me anything about what you saw out there?"

"I was using the binoculars, which we'd brought on account of the whales, you see. Wayne said it was silly for me to be using them there because there were no whales yet, but then I saw the guy with the lobster trap. I thought it was interesting, so I started watching him, didn't I? And it was the strangest thing. I said to Wayne, 'What is he putting in that trap? It doesn't look like bait to me.' He said he was sure it was fine, but then I read about the stolen art that turned up in a trap. I just know I saw him!"

"Can you tell me more about where you were when this happened?"

"I'm not so good with that kind of thing. We were out of the marina, for sure, because the boat goes much faster once you're out of the marina. It was maybe half an hour or forty minutes into the ride. We hadn't seen any whales yet though."

"Can you describe what you saw him putting into the trap?"

"It was a black box of some kind, the size of a shoebox." That was about the size of the plastic container that had held the bust. "I thought it was strange. Wayne said I didn't know anything about lobsters, so how would I know what would be strange or not? But now I'm the one who saw the thief, aren't I?"

"Can you describe the thief?"

"He was a man, and he wore a T-shirt, a hat, and sunglasses."

"So you couldn't see his face?"

"Afraid not. We weren't all that close, and he was covered up, so I couldn't see much even with the binoculars. It was so bright that I didn't think anything of him wearing a hat and glasses."

"What about the boat? Can you tell me anything about that?"

"Not really, I'm afraid. I don't know much about boats. I think it was white."

So were many of the boats Harriet had seen, so that wasn't much help. But she had an idea. "Did you take any pictures?"

"I took lots of pictures, but mostly they're of the water. Those whales don't make it easy to get pictures of them, let me tell you."

"Did you get any pictures of the man with the lobster trap, I mean?"

"Oh. No, I'm afraid not. I was using the binoculars, so I didn't have the camera handy."

That was too bad. But still, what Barbara had told her was better than nothing. "Is there anything else you can tell me about the man you saw?"

"Not that I can think of. I've told you everything I told the police. Hey, is there a reward out? Like, for information?"

"Not that I know of," Harriet said. "But if I do hear of anything like that, I'll be sure to let you know."

"Great. I could use a holiday. Lisa told me about these cute little cottages up in the lake district that sound so nice."

"Thank you for your help."

Harriet ended the call, mulling over what she'd learned. Not a lot, she finally decided. Barbara might have seen the thief depositing the art into the lobster trap, but she couldn't describe him or the boat he'd been on, so what good was that?

She clicked over to her email and saw the usual—newsletters, headlines, appeals for money. There were a couple emails from friends back home, which she read greedily and marked as unread so she wouldn't forget to reply to them.

And then she saw one from Oscar Ramirez, the former guard at the Atkinson Museum. She clicked on the email.

I thought this might interest you. From the one camera that was working. —O

Harriet opened the attached video and soon realized it was security footage of the room in the museum where the Norse coins had been kept. The date stamp on it was the day the coins were taken.

She frowned. Was it even legal for him to send the footage to her? But, well, it was here, so she might as well see what was on it.

She watched a couple of guests wander into the room, browse the artifacts there, and then leave. After that, there was no movement for several minutes. Harriet sped up the footage, and still nothing happened.

Until shortly after three, according to the time stamp, when Oscar came into the room, likely on his rounds. He walked into the room, scanned it, and then walked out. A family walked through a while later, the young children clearly bored by the experience, and then they all went out the side door.

Ten minutes later, another person walked into the room. He wore a fedora, sunglasses, and a scarf pulled up over the bottom half of his face. She paused the footage. This must be their guy. Did he walk through the whole museum like that? How had the guards and volunteers not immediately been struck by his suspicious appearance?

She studied him, trying to make out any hint of who he was in the grainy black-and-white footage. He wore dark colors, dark shoes, and a dark hat. He was covered up well. It could be Johnny. But there wasn't any way to know for sure, or to prove it.

She pressed play on the video, and the man walked straight to the glass case where the coins were displayed. He didn't hesitate, but brazenly lifted the lid of the case and set it on the floor. He'd known it wasn't alarmed then. He pulled a small bag from a pocket in his coat, slid the coins inside, and tucked the pouch back into the pocket. Then he put the lid back on the case and walked coolly out of the room.

Harriet let out a long breath. She couldn't believe it. This was the theft, caught on camera. She watched the footage again, hoping to spot something she'd missed. She did notice that the man managed to keep his face turned away from the corner where the working camera was, as if he knew about the actual security.

And it would make sense if he had, because he also somehow knew about the case not being alarmed. Whoever this guy was, he was brazen—stealing the coins like that in the middle of a museum gallery, where guests could wander in at any time—and knowledgeable about what he was doing. He knew where the security flaws were and how to exploit them.

So who was he?

Harriet watched the video one more time and then finally gave up and pushed herself out of her chair. The trained professionals hadn't been able to identify the man in the days since the theft. How did she think she would do so? But still, a part of her had hoped.

She got dressed and ready for her day, moved the laundry to the dryer, and then went over to the clinic. There were only a few patients that morning, so they were able to close early when the last dog left. Polly said goodbye and headed home, and Harriet went back to her house and changed before she set out for a trip to town. She was finally going to get groceries.

A few minutes later, Harriet pushed her cart—or trolley, as the locals called it—down the aisle of the grocery store. She was halfway through the frozen-food section when her phone rang. It was an unknown number, but a local one.

"Hello?"

"Hello, is this Harriet Bailey?"

"Speaking."

"This is Mary Holcombe, from the Heritage Commission." Judging by the voice and the precise, clipped syllables, Harriet guessed she was an older woman with an upscale background.

"Oh. Yes. Hello." Harriet was surprised that she was calling on a Saturday. But maybe preserving the region's heritage was a job that didn't have weekends off. "Thank you for calling back. I was hoping to speak to David from your team."

"Yes, that's what I'm calling you about," Mary said. "I wanted to ask you to check the name. There's no David who works at this office."

"There's not?" But David was the name Mrs. Lewis had given her, wasn't it?

"No, I'm afraid not. But is there someone else who might be able to help?"

Harriet thought quickly. "Can you tell me if anyone from the Heritage Commission has been out to Beresford Manor in the past several months?"

Harriet stepped out of the way so a man could grab frozen pizzas from the case in front of her.

"Beresford Manor? That's a lovely home. Let me see." Harriet could hear keys clicking in the background. "No one from our office has visited the property in the past six months."

"So no one came to inspect the repair to the woodwork around a window?"

"There was a repair to a window? No one notified us about that. Is the window visible from the exterior of the house?"

"I really don't know." Harriet suddenly worried she'd gotten Liam and Mrs. Lewis in trouble. "But in any case, you're sure no one has been there and there's no David at your office?"

"I'm very sure." Her voice was now huffy, her hackles up.

"Is there any chance someone named David works for another branch of the Heritage Commission?"

"This is the only office certified to inspect and certify homes in Yorkshire," she said, her voice cold. "I assure you that I know all the people in this office and there is no David."

"Thank you. I appreciate your help." Harriet ended the call and immediately pulled up Mrs. Lewis's number.

"Hello, Harriet."

"Hi, Mrs. Lewis. I'm sorry to bother you, but I wanted to check on something. You told me someone named David from the Heritage Commission was in the house last month to inspect the repair work to the window. Is that right?"

"Yes. It was quite annoying, to tell you the truth. I hadn't even filed the paperwork to report the repair yet, and someone was already at my door. They want you to report these things right away or they threaten to slap you with fines. They have eyes everywhere, I tell you."

Alarm bells went off in Harriet's head. "You're saying you hadn't even filed the report, but someone came to inspect the repair anyway?"

"Right. Somehow they knew. One of their spies told them, no doubt. Always trying to catch the owners out."

"Is it possible it wasn't actually someone from the Heritage Commission?"

"I don't—" She broke off. "Oh my. I don't know."

"Did he show you any identification or anything? Any way to prove he was who he said he was?"

"I'm afraid not. I didn't think to ask. Who would impersonate someone from the Heritage Commission? It would never occur to me."

"I just spoke with someone at the commission, and she told me there's no one named David who works from that office. They didn't send anyone to inspect the house, and they didn't know about the repair. Although I should tell you that they're aware of it now," Harriet said sheepishly. "I'm sorry about that."

"It's hardly your fault, dear. You're saying that the person who came here and told me he was from the Heritage Commission—that's probably who stole that bust?"

"Was he alone in the house at any point?"

"Yes, of course. I don't follow them around when they're here. I'd never seen this inspector before, but he seemed to know where he was going, so I let him be." She let out a groan. "What was I thinking?"

"What do you remember about him?" Harriet asked. "Anything stand out?"

"Nothing remarkable, or I would have remembered," Mrs. Lewis said. "Let me think. He reminded me of my James, when he was young. My husband was quite a looker, let me tell you. Every girl in town chased him. Marjorie Allers never spoke to me again after I started dating him."

"What color hair did 'David' have?" Harriet asked, trying to get the conversation back on track.

"Lots of floppy brown hair. Kind of curly, you know?" Johnny had brown hair, but it wasn't floppy or curly. Then again, he could have been wearing a wig. "He had a mustache too. I know that because I remember thinking he should shave it off. It added ten years to him."

Johnny also didn't have a mustache. But neither did Shane O'Grady or anyone else she'd spoken to. Facial hair was easy to change. "Was he young?"

"Oh yes. But then, everyone looks young to me these days."

"If you had to guess his age, what would you say?"

"Honestly, I'm awful at judging these things. Twenties or thirties, probably? Certainly no older than my daughter, that's for sure. And she's thirty-eight."

"That's great. That's very helpful." There was a big difference between twenty—Johnny's age—and thirty-eight, but Mrs. Lewis had said she was bad at judging. It could be him. Or it could have been someone working with him. "What was he wearing?"

"I don't know. A button-down, probably, and trousers of some kind."

Harriet did her best to keep her frustration out of her tone. "Can you think of anything else about him that stands out?"

"I'm afraid not. I was hoping to get rid of him as quickly as possible. I didn't spend much time studying him."

Now that Harriet thought about it, that was probably by design. It was clever of the intruder to disguise himself as a nondescript version of someone Mrs. Lewis wouldn't want to spend time with. "If you think of anything, please let me know."

"Of course."

Harriet hung up and realized she was shivering, and it wasn't because she was still in the middle of the frozen-foods aisle. The thief had been there, in the house, and Mrs. Lewis had interacted with him. She talked to him.

But who was he? Harriet wasn't sure she was any closer to finding the answer.

CHAPTER NINETEEN

Harriet was on her way home from the grocery store when her phone rang again. This time she recognized the number that popped up on the screen. She put the call on speaker and answered right away.

"Hi, Claire."

"Hey there. Desmond has worked his magic. Any chance you're free to stop by and check it out?"

"Absolutely. I've got a car full of groceries at the moment, but how about I drop them off and come over after that?"

"That sounds great. We'll see you soon."

Harriet carried the groceries inside the house and put them away. She went out into the yard and tossed a ball for Maxwell, who ran after it eagerly for several minutes. When he started slowing down, Harriet brought him inside and refilled his water and food dishes. He slurped up water then walked to his bed. She removed his wheels so he could settle in for a nice long nap.

Harriet patted Charlie, who glared at her. "I love you too, Charlie," she said, scratching the cat under the chin before she headed out.

Aunt Jinny was working in her yard. She spotted Harriet and beckoned. Harriet immediately ducked into the lush oasis of her aunt's garden.

"Have any plans this evening?" Aunt Jinny asked.

"Not really. Will has a new-members class."

"Want to come over for dinner? I'm making tomato soup, and the recipe makes way too much for one person."

"I'd love to."

"Perfect. I'll see you around six?"

"I'm looking forward to it."

There were plenty of people out and about on this sunny May day, and it made Harriet happy to see so many people walking through the streets and enjoying the beautiful weather. She pulled up in front of Claire's house a few minutes later.

Claire opened the door. "Come on in. Excuse the mess. It's been a full week around here." She kicked a pair of cleats aside, picked up a fallen baseball bat, and leaned it up against the wall. "Desmond's in his room."

Harriet followed Claire down the hall and into a bedroom that was dominated by a desk laden with computer equipment. Two large monitors were surrounded by keyboards and controllers and other computer things Harriet couldn't identify.

Desmond sat in a rolling chair, headphones over his ears. He took them off when Harriet and his mother walked into the room.

Claire opened the blinds, filling the room with sunlight, and then cracked the window. "Can you show Harriet what you found, Des?"

"Sure." He closed whatever game he was playing and pulled up another window. Harriet didn't recognize the program, but it appeared to be photo editing software. The image of Johnny pulling up the lobster trap was on the screen. "This is the photo as it appeared on social media, right?"

"That looks right," Harriet said, squinting. There was Johnny, hoisting the trap, the water turquoise around him. And there were the buoys, orange and blue, bobbing along the water's surface.

"Well, here is it with the filters removed," Desmond said, pulling up another version of the photo. It was decidedly less bright, and somehow seemed to have less life in it. The colors were duller, the sky grayer, the water dark. And—

"Oh." The buoys were definitely red and blue. "Can you show me the other one again?"

Desmond switched back and forth between the versions a few times to show her the difference. "The buoys appear orange because of the filter that was used, but they're actually red."

Johnny had been telling the truth. This wasn't a picture of him pulling up lobster traps where the artifacts were found.

"Does that help?" Desmond asked.

"It does," Harriet confirmed. "You did a great job."

"Are you sure?" Claire asked her. "You don't sound too happy."

"This sets my investigation back," Harriet admitted.

"Oh, I'm sorry."

"You don't need to be sorry," Harriet said. "I want to know the truth, even if it doesn't align with my theories. *Especially* if it doesn't align with my theories."

"I was able to use the metadata in the file to geolocate the position of the photo as well," Desmond said. He clicked into another program and pulled up a map. "The picture was taken here," he said, indicating an area of the map south of the harbor. "The trap with the contraband was found up here, right?" He pointed to an area north of the harbor.

"Further proof that this isn't the same trap," Harriet said.

He nodded. "The metadata doesn't lie."

"Well, I'm glad to know that," Harriet said. It didn't mean Johnny hadn't been involved in putting the stolen goods in the trap. It just meant that this photo didn't show him doing so. "Thanks for your help."

"Sure thing," the boy replied.

"Five more minutes, and then it's time to come out and fold the laundry," Claire told him.

"Okay, Mum." Desmond slipped his headphones back over his ears.

Claire led Harriet out to the kitchen, where they chatted for a few minutes about a new couple at church and Claire's preparations for the upcoming church picnic. Then Harriet thanked her and headed home.

It had already been quite a day. She'd learned that the person who'd stolen Liam's bust had impersonated a Heritage Commission employee, she'd seen the security camera footage of the theft of the coins, she'd learned that Johnny Bradley told her the truth about the photo of the lobster trap, and she'd also learned that whoever placed the artifacts inside the trap might have been spotted by at least one person on a whale-watching cruise.

If there was a photo that captured him doing that, she could compare it to the image of the guy in the security camera footage and see how that lined up with the description of the guy who'd come to Beresford Manor. If only...

And then Harriet had an idea. Just because Barbara Greeley didn't take a photo didn't mean no one did.

As soon as Harriet got home, she opened her laptop and pulled up the website for the whale-watching tour company again. *#WhitbyWhaleWatchTours* was splashed across the top of the page, reminding customers to use the hashtag when they posted their photos online.

Harriet wasn't a huge social media user, but she knew enough to understand that if someone included a hashtag in their post, anyone who looked up that hashtag could find the post. She opened up her social media page and did a search for *#WhitbyWhaleWatchTours*. Her screen filled with images posted by different people.

There were some great shots of whales breaching and humpbacks slapping the water with their big fins. Other images showed dolphins flying in and out of the water alongside the boat. Harriet hadn't realized dolphins lived so far north. There were some beautiful pictures of the craggy coastline from the sea, the sheer rock faces tall and austere. There were also photos of the water, a lighthouse at the end of a long pier, and different groups of people posing on boats. Some of the photos obviously had filters applied, while others didn't appear to have been doctored.

There were pages and pages of results. She clicked on the first few and saw that they were roughly in order, with the most recent photos showing first. Harriet scrolled through dozens of them until she came to pictures posted the previous Saturday. Those must be from the tour Barbara and her husband were on. Harriet scrolled through photos of beaches, open water, groups posing on the deck, whales, and—

Wait. Harriet clicked on a photo that showed a smaller boat surrounded by buoys. Buoys that appeared to have navy blue and orange stripes. And a man at the back of the boat hoisting what looked to be a lobster trap out of the water. The caption read, *Does it get any better than this? It's almost like they paid him to make this trip feel more authentic. I can't imagine a more perfect seaside town.* #WhitbyWhaleWatchTours.

Harriet studied the photo. It was as Barbara had described. The man wore a hat and glasses, and there was very little she could tell about him. He was alone on the boat, hoisting up the cage, and his face was turned away from the camera.

She examined his clothing, but he wore what appeared to be a plain white T-shirt and khaki shorts. He was reasonably fit and apparently strong enough to manage the heavy trap alone, but beyond that she could see no identifying marks, no logo on his shirt or hat. She scanned for visible tattoos but didn't see any of those either.

But there was a dark box in the bottom of the lobster trap he balanced on the edge of the boat.

It could be the same guy from the security camera footage. It could be the same person Mrs. Lewis had seen and the one who came into the marina office and applied for the permit in Myles's name. But there was no way to know for sure, and no way to identify him—at least that she could see.

The boat appeared to be a regular-size, white boat. Maybe Will would be able to tell her more about it, but from what she could see it was just a boat like any other. Having grown up in Connecticut, Harriet was familiar with sailboats, pontoons, and fishing boats, but she wasn't well-versed in the finer points about any of them.

She wondered if the boat had a name. That would certainly make it easier to find. Then she spotted letters and numbers on the side of the boat: WY754. Some kind of registration number? Perhaps it could be used to trace the owner of the boat.

Was this the same boat that Johnny was on in the other photo? If it was—if she could make this connection—she would have the evidence she needed. She pulled up that photo and compared the boats.

It was actually really hard to tell. The picture from the whale tour showed the side of the boat, while the picture of Johnny showed a view looking over the back of the vessel and out to the water beyond. She couldn't see the part where the number would have been at all. They might be the same boat, but based on what she could see here, there was no way to know. Which meant that Johnny had just jumped to the top of her suspect list again.

She picked up her phone and called Will. He didn't answer. He was probably in the middle of the new-members class.

Could she figure this out herself? Harriet found a watercraft registration site, but it didn't seem to be searchable. If she could just figure out who the boat was registered to—

She jumped when her phone rang. Will. She picked up at once. "How can you tell who a boat is registered to?"

"What?"

"I'm sorry. I mean, how's your day been? Is the class going well?"

Will chuckled. "It's great. They're good people. Now what's this about boat registration?"

"I found a picture of the guy with the lobster trap. The one Barbara told me about."

"Wait, you talked to Barbara? The one who posted the comment on the newspaper article?"

She realized how much she had to tell him. "Yes, it's been a fruitful day. Barbara described the man she saw on the whale-watching tour as well as she could, but she didn't have a picture of him. But then I found one online—"

"All the fun stuff happens while I'm stuck in church meetings," Will joked.

"Important church meetings," Harriet said. "We're excited about new members, remember?"

"I am excited, but I also need to know what's happened while I've been talking through the volunteer and service opportunities at the church."

"How much time do you have?"

"About two minutes."

"The full update will have to wait then. For now, I have a photo that I think shows our thief in the act of depositing the stolen goods in the trap, but there's nothing to identify him. However, there's a clear shot of the letters and numbers on the side of the boat, so I'm trying to find out what they mean."

"That's probably the PLN, the port letters and numbers. There should be one to three letters at the beginning."

Harriet checked. "Yep. WY."

"That identifies the port of registration, which, in this case, is Whitby."

"Oh, of course. Then there are three numbers."

"Those should identify the owner of the vessel."

"I tried searching online, but I didn't get anywhere."

Will hummed in thought. "In that case, you may need to go down to the marina and ask at the office. I'm sure they have access to the registration records. However, I'm not sure if those numbers are a matter of public record. They may only be able to tell the police."

"I'll go find out."

"Can it wait until I'm done here?"

Harriet chuckled. "You really don't want to miss out on the fun, do you?"

"I really don't."

"Go hang out with the new members. I'll keep you posted." She threw on her shoes and rushed out, even though saving two minutes would hardly make a difference in getting the information she wanted.

The drive to Whitby was becoming familiar, and Harriet made it mostly on autopilot. The parking lot at the marina was pretty full, and on any other day, Harriet would have enjoyed standing at the edge of a dock and watching the boats go in and out of the harbor, but today she headed directly for the office.

Her heart sank as she approached the small wooden building. The lights were off inside. Could it really be closed? She tried the door, but it was locked. On a beautiful sunny weekend day in May when marina traffic was higher than ever? Sure enough, a sign on the door said that they were open Monday through Friday.

Harriet wanted to bang her head against a wall. How had she not thought to check the hours online before making the drive here? Would she have to wait until Monday to find out who owned the boat?

She looked around. There wasn't anyone she could ask, at least not as far as she could tell. She would have to wait.

Though, actually, Will had suggested that the police might have access to the information she wanted. Maybe they'd already found the photo from the tour themselves and were tracking things down. But she should probably alert them to what she'd found out anyway.

She dialed Van, and twice he made her repeat the steps she'd taken to find the picture. When he'd found it online himself and noted the numbers on the hull of the boat, he promised to check them right away. She hung up, knowing she'd done the right thing, but she was still unsettled. Hopefully the police would have more luck than she had. Hopefully they would be able to find the owner of the boat and have the man in custody before the office opened on Monday.

Hopefully.

All she could do was wait.

CHAPTER TWENTY

Harriet spent the rest of the day cleaning the house, taking a walk along the cliffs, and putting together a salad to take to Aunt Jinny's house for dinner. She was unsettled, both by the events of the day and—whenever she could stop thinking about the boat and the security camera footage—by the thought of meeting Dustin the next day. Why had he come all the way to England? Why couldn't he leave the past in the past? She wondered if it was too late to cancel.

By the time she headed over to Aunt Jinny's house, all she wanted to do was go to bed and skip the following day altogether.

"What's going on?" Aunt Jinny asked the moment Harriet stepped through the door. She took the salad bowl from Harriet's hands. "What's wrong?" Aunt Jinny's house was warm and welcoming, with the windows open to let in the fresh air and cheerful curtains on the windows. She led Harriet into the cozy kitchen and set the bowl on the counter.

"Nothing's wrong."

Her aunt snorted. "I've known you since you were in diapers, child. I can tell when something is bothering you. Tell me what's going on. Is it this stolen art thing still? Matilda told me she had a lovely visit with you."

"Matilda was great," Harriet said. "She was very helpful. And the stolen art is part of what's bothering me. It's been kind of a wild day."

"Tell me about it." Aunt Jinny placed a cup of tea in her hands—Harriet didn't even know where it had come from—and indicated she should sit at the kitchen table. "What have you found out?"

Harriet recounted her day, updated her aunt on what she'd learned in the past few days, and finished with what she was waiting for the police to find out.

"It sounds like you're getting very close," Aunt Jinny said. "If the police are able to identify the owner of that boat or identify the man in the security camera footage, then you're in business. And you think it's this university kid?"

"I can't see who else it would be."

"You don't think Shane O'Grady is involved?"

"I don't know. He could be. But I haven't found any way he's connected to Johnny or Riley, and he wasn't the one on the boat." She pulled up the photo on her phone. "See?"

Aunt Jinny studied the screen. "No, I suppose it's not. That's someone much younger than Shane."

"I'm not saying he couldn't have been involved. But if this is the man who put the stolen goods in the trap, it wasn't Shane."

"So who else do you have who's younger than Shane?"

"Just Johnny, really. I'm trying to figure out if this is the same boat as the one that shows Johnny checking the lobster trap in this picture. I know they're not the same traps—I've already looked into that—but is it the same boat?" She pulled up the social media photo of Johnny and showed it to her aunt.

Aunt Jinny flipped back and forth between the photos. "It seems like it could be the same boat."

"Right?"

"But it could also not. You can't see enough of it to be sure either way."

"Exactly."

"Well, keep working at it," Aunt Jinny said. "You always do manage to find the answer to puzzles like this eventually, don't you?"

"I've gotten lucky a few times," Harriet admitted. "But this one even has the police stumped, as far as I can tell."

"Don't forget to ask the Lord for wisdom," Aunt Jinny said. "He gives graciously to all who ask."

It was a reminder Harriet needed and could never hear too many times. "Thank you."

Aunt Jinny ladled out the tomato soup and carried the bowls to the table to join a loaf of fresh bread and tall glasses of the drink Harriet knew as lemonade, though in the UK it was called "lemon drink." What they called lemonade was a carbonated beverage.

Harriet set the salad on the table, and they sat down.

Aunt Jinny blessed the meal, and then, after Harriet took the first wonderfully flavorful sip of her soup, her aunt asked, "What else is bothering you?"

Harriet knew better than to try to keep something from her aunt. "I'm meeting Dustin for lunch tomorrow."

Aunt Jinny nearly dropped her spoon. "Dustin is coming to White Church Bay?"

"He is."

"Why?"

"I don't know. He wants to talk to me. At first I said no, but then Polly and Claire said I should hear him out. Polly thinks he's going to ask me to get back together with him."

"And if he does?" Aunt Jinny looked at her over the rim of her water glass.

Harriet didn't have to think about it. "I would say no. I've moved on. I love Will."

Aunt Jinny dipped a chunk of bread in her soup. "Old flames can be very tempting. It's easy to fall into the trap of imagining you can rekindle what you once had."

"It's not tempting for me," Harriet said firmly. "I don't want that again. Even if I wasn't with Will, I know now that Dustin and I weren't right for each other. I doubt that's changed. Besides, my life is here now."

"I'm glad to hear it. And I hope, for your sake and his, that's not why he's come all this way."

Harriet set her spoon down and examined her aunt's expression. "You sound like you don't think that's it anyway."

Aunt Jinny flapped a hand. "Oh, I don't know. I obviously have no clue what's going through his mind. I just wonder."

"Wonder what?"

Aunt Jinny stirred her soup. "It's been quite a while since he broke up with you and you moved here. A lot has changed for you in that time. I guess I imagine a lot has changed for him as well."

"What do you mean?"

"You've grown a lot since you broke up, so it's reasonable to think he has too. I'll be interested to see if that shows in whatever he's come to say."

Harriet felt silly for a moment. Of course Dustin was different now than he'd been when she left, though she was ashamed to admit she hadn't really thought about that until Aunt Jinny pointed it out. In her mind, Dustin was frozen in time, the same person he'd been when he'd unceremoniously dumped her, but of course he wasn't. The intervening months must have affected him too. He must have changed. Maybe, as Aunt Jinny suggested, even grown.

"Do you think he's coming to apologize?" Harriet read between the lines of what her aunt was suggesting.

"I have no idea." She popped the bread in her mouth and chewed, and then, eventually, said, "One can hope."

What if he *had* come to apologize? She couldn't imagine it, but she supposed it was possible. What would she do? She would have to accept it, wouldn't she? Did she want to? He'd broken her heart and made it impossible for her to continue her career back in the States, since they'd worked in the same clinic. How did one forgive something like that?

As if she knew what Harriet was thinking, Aunt Jinny met her gaze. "I'll be praying for you."

CHAPTER TWENTY-ONE

arriet woke early Sunday morning, groggy from a restless night. After lying awake for several hours with thoughts swirling in her mind, she'd managed to fall asleep shortly before the alarm went off. She fed the animals then made a pot of coffee and sat down with her Bible. She prayed for Will and for Aunt Jinny, for her family in Connecticut, and that the Lord would bless whatever happened that day.

The sky was cloudy and the air cool when she went out to let Maxwell run around. When she came back in, she poured another cup of coffee and settled in front of her laptop to scan her email. Newsletters, advertising, more of the same old same old.

And an email from Mason McGinnis. Was this the real Mason McGinnis? Or the fake one? Why would either of them be sending her a message? She opened the email, noting that it came from his real address.

Harriet,

I've been slowly catching up on my inbox, which was sorely neglected while I was overseas. I finally dug back far enough that I found the emails sent shortly after I left, and I discovered this. Trenton has a gallery in London, and I've worked with him a few times. *I don't know if there's any con-nection to the pieces you were asking about, but I thought it might be worth forwarding along, just in case.*

Harriet scrolled down the email to find a message from some-one named Trenton White.

Mason,

I hope all is well. I have a foreign collector interested in pieces from the prehistoric and early modern periods. Stone Age, Bronze Age, Roman, Anglo-Saxon—really anything very old would work. Money is no object for the right piece, and he's not picky about provenance. If you know of anything that might fit the bill, please let me know.

—TW

Harriet reread the email. *Not picky about provenance* was basi-cally code for *doesn't care how the pieces are acquired or whether it's even legal.* The time periods mentioned could also be the link between the stolen artifacts she'd been searching for.

The original email had been sent to Mason back in early March. Was this Trenton White connected to the fake Mason? Were they the same person?

Harriet ran a search for the name Trenton White and found several pages of results. The first was the website for a gallery in London called White Projects, *the premier gallery for the discerning collector, featuring the works of today's most important artists and the most significant pieces from our past.*

The photos showed white gallery walls covered with bright, colorful abstract paintings, as well as some antiques and artifacts. The website was slick and well-designed, and the About Us page featured a picture of a man with a wide smile and red hair.

Harriet read the bio beneath the photo, which boasted of Trenton's education at various elite institutions, his experience working at several galleries in London, Hong Kong, and New York, and his successful career working with famous artists. She assumed they must be famous artists, judging by the way they were tossed out in the bio as if their names commanded respect.

She studied the photo of Trenton. His skin was pale, his eyes light blue. Martina at the marina office had said the man who'd applied for the permit in Myles's name had brown hair. Mrs. Lewis said the same thing about the man who posed as someone from the Heritage Commission. But anyone could put on a wig. And it was impossible to tell much about the man on the boat in the photo from the whale tour. Maybe it was Trenton.

She poked around on the page for more information, but of course there was nothing about dealing in stolen artifacts or sourcing art for buyers with deep pockets and limited concern about ethics.

She clicked back to the main search page and began to sort through the other results. There were pictures of Trenton White at parties and on society pages. There were stories about big deals he'd facilitated in the art world. There was a profile of him, his beautiful wife, and their adorable children in the lifestyle section of a newspaper in London. There was no obvious connection to White Church Bay or to lobsters, but that didn't mean there wasn't one.

Harriet noticed the time with a start. She would be late for church if she didn't get going soon. She knew the police needed to see what she'd found, so she forwarded the email to Van, and then she hurried to get ready, spending a bit of extra time making sure her hair was smooth and her dress flattering. She would meet up with Dustin for lunch after church, and she wanted to feel as confident as she could for that meeting.

Will preached from the book of Jonah, and Harriet had never appreciated that passage more. She was also facing a task she didn't want to do, but she knew she couldn't run from it the way Jonah had run from the assignment in Nineveh.

And, watching Will up there at the front of the church, she could see how much he loved teaching the congregation about the Lord and what His Word meant for them, and she was filled with awe and gratitude that she got to be a part of his life. He loved the Lord and His church, and he loved her. She didn't know how she'd gotten so blessed.

After the service, Harriet drank tea and chatted with several of the regulars. All too soon, it was time to go meet up with Dustin. She said goodbye to Will, who promised to pray for her, and then she drove to town.

She stepped into the Crow's Nest, and there he was, standing inside the door. He looked as she remembered—brown hair in a trendy style, brown eyes, high cheekbones. He smiled at her, and suddenly all her worry and fears melted away. She'd thought she would feel nothing but anger and hurt and confusion, all the things she'd felt in the months after he broke off their engagement, but actually, it felt like seeing an old friend. She realized she was glad to see him.

"Hello, Dustin."

"Harriet." He reached out his arms and gave her a hug, and the smell of his spicy cologne took her back to when they'd first started dating and she'd found the scent intoxicating. Now it just seemed pleasant. "It's good to see you again."

She returned his smile, taking him in. "You look well." She meant it. His cheeks were pink, and his eyes had lost the wretched expression they'd had in the last few months of their relationship. She could see now that he hadn't been well toward the end of their engagement.

"So do you." He gestured. "Should we grab a seat?"

They found a table tucked in the corner of the room, and she walked him through some of the dishes she enjoyed and thought he might as well.

He grinned at her. "You sound like you've been here all your life. I can't believe this is where you live now. White Church Bay is so charming. I got here early, so I stopped in at a bookstore and got a coffee at that tearoom. It's like something out of a movie. It's unreal."

"It really is a beautiful place," Harriet said. "Sometimes I have to pinch myself so I know I'm not dreaming."

"It feels like someone imagined the archetypal English village and then built it."

"It does have that quality," Harriet agreed.

"And how's the vet practice? Is that going well?"

"It's good, and I have quite a variety. I get to work on large animals—lots of sheep and horses, an occasional llama—as well as pets. My grandfather built up a solid business, and it's worked out well for me to step into it. People weren't sure at first that I could fill his shoes, but they've come around."

"I have no doubt. Is it strange living in his house?"

"Actually, it's wonderful. It helps me feel close to him, and I love being so near my aunt."

"I'm glad." He smiled, and she knew he was telling the truth. He was happy for her, and Aunt Jinny had been right. Something about Dustin was different. There was a peace about him that she hadn't seen in years. He wasn't trying to impress her. He was asking because he genuinely wanted to know.

"And how about you?" Harriet asked. "How are things with you? How's the office?"

"The office is fine," he said. "The new vet we hired when you left is efficient and knows what she's doing, but she's not overly friendly. It doesn't impact the quality of her work, but it's obviously not the same."

A waitress came and took their order, and Harriet ordered a salad while Dustin got a burger.

"And how about your life?" Harriet asked.

"I'm doing well," Dustin said. "That's actually what I want to talk to you about. Things are really good. Totally different than when we were together. I have a good therapist who's helped me realize how many things I was doing wrong. I've been sleeping and exercising more, and just generally trying to not be so self-centered. I feel like a different person. I wasn't in a good place, as I'm sure you know. I couldn't be a good business partner or fiancé to you because I was working through too many things of my own, and I know now that you paid the price for my immaturity. But it's different now, and so I knew I needed to come here to ask you something."

Harriet froze. Was he about to ask her to give their relationship another try? As happy as she was that he was doing better, she had no desire to get back together with him. She was happy here, with her friends, her life, her work—and Will.

"What's that?" she made herself ask. She braced for the words she didn't want to hear. Things were going well so far, but if she had to turn him down, it was sure to turn ugly, and—

"I want to ask you to forgive me."

Aunt Jinny had been right, but Harriet was still surprised. "What?"

"I'm asking you to forgive me," he said. "I treated you terribly, Harriet. I acted out of my own immaturity and pain. I wasn't ready to get married, but I didn't want to lose you. So I proposed, even though I wasn't in a place to be in a healthy relationship with you. It was selfish of me to toy with your emotions like that and put my own wants above your needs—which was further proof that I wasn't ready to get married. I know that when I broke things off, I hurt you deeply. And I am so sorry."

Harriet couldn't believe it. She'd never had such a conversation with Dustin before. She'd never seen him like this. He really *had* changed.

He seemed to misunderstand her silence. "It's all right if you can't forgive me. I would completely understand. But I wanted to say it, and I hope someday you'll be able to forgive me for the pain and hurt I caused you, for yourself and for the peace you deserve."

"Th-thank you," she stammered. She hoped she could forgive him too, though she didn't know if she could get there in the next few minutes. "That means a lot."

"Seeing you here, seeing how happy you are in your new home, makes me even more glad I came," he said. "I know that, as painful as it was, the move was right for you. I can see that you're happier now than you ever were with me. I own up to being responsible for a lot of your unhappiness, of course, but I also don't think you were as fulfilled there as you deserve to be."

Harriet couldn't deny it. There was a time when she had loved her life back in Connecticut, but it had been a few years since she'd felt the kind of joy she felt every day in White Church Bay.

The waitress set their food in front of them and checked to see if they needed anything else, and then she hurried away.

"There was something else I wanted to tell you," Dustin said.

Harriet braced herself again, afraid that the peace that had settled over them was about to shatter. "Yes?"

He took a deep breath and let it out and then took a sip of his water and swallowed. Harriet felt her anxiety ramp up with every second that passed.

Finally, he said, "I've met someone. Her name is Maddie. She's an elementary school teacher. She's kind and smart and wonderful."

Harriet sat with that news for a moment, waiting to feel jealous or upset or anything else. But she didn't. "I'm happy for you."

"She's made me see—well, all kinds of things, honestly, but also just how wrong I was for you."

Harriet couldn't disagree with him there. She had realized the same thing through her relationship with Will. "We were wrong for each other."

"We were," he agreed. "And it's serious between Maddie and me. However, before I move forward with her, I need to make things right with you."

Harriet wasn't sure how to respond. Was he asking her to be okay with him proposing to Maddie? Was she okay with that if that's what he wanted to do?

She considered his words, and suddenly she felt as if a weight had been lifted from her shoulders. She hadn't realized how afraid she'd been that he'd come to ask her to give him another shot. Now that she knew what he was really thinking, she didn't feel sad or disappointed. She felt relief. She felt oddly free.

"I'm happy for you," she said. "And I'm glad you did this. Thank you for coming here to tell me. I wish you and Maddie nothing but the best."

It felt weird to tell the man she'd once thought she would marry that she wanted him to be happy with someone else. But it was true, and she could see his face relax as she said it.

"Actually, I've met someone also," she went on. "He's the pastor of the church here, and I think it may be serious too." At least, she knew it was serious on her side, and she thought it was on Will's as well.

"That's great. I'm glad." He smiled at her. "I wish you nothing but the best, Harriet. I hope he's better to you than I ever could have been."

Harriet didn't know what the future would hold with Will, but after her conversation with Dustin, she felt liberated. What had happened with him was truly and completely in the past. That door was closed. And while a year ago that realization probably would have made her sad, now she felt hopeful and optimistic. She could stop looking back and focus on the future.

And she had to believe there were good things to come. Thinking about Will, she was sure of it.

CHAPTER TWENTY-TWO

Harriet ate dinner with Will that night, and he was visibly relieved when she told him what Dustin had come to Yorkshire to say. He never came out and said it, but it was clear he'd been worried that Dustin wanted to ask her to try again and that she might agree because of the history between them.

"I told him I was seeing someone and that it was serious," Harriet said.

In answer, Will took her hand and threaded his fingers between hers. She wanted him to never let go.

She slept well and deeply Sunday night, and when the alarm went off on Monday morning, she could hardly believe it was time to get up. She rolled out of bed and felt well rested for the first time in a while.

A glance at her calendar told Harriet she had some time before her first appointment of the day. She got in the Land Rover and drove straight to the marina, where she found the office lit and unlocked. She walked in to find Martina sitting at her desk.

Martina raised her head. "Hello. Did you have any luck with that lobster trap?"

"I may be getting closer. I was wondering if you might be able to help me again."

"Sure. What do you need?"

When Harriet explained that she wanted to search for a boat registration number, Martina made a face. "I can help with that, but it could take several days to get the information."

"There's no online database?" Harriet asked.

"I can request it, but it always takes a while for them to get back to me," Martina explained.

"Well, whenever you're able to get it, I would appreciate it," Harriet said. She assumed the police must not have gotten to the marina yet to ask for the same information.

"I'll see what I can do," Martina assured her.

"I have another question," Harriet said. She showed Martina the picture of Johnny. "Is this the guy who came in to register for the license in Myles's name?"

Martina took the phone and zoomed in on the photo. "Maybe? I can't tell. It could be. But it also might not be. I'm really sorry. I know that doesn't help you. But I can't point fingers if I'm not sure, you know."

"I understand." Harriet fought down her frustration and showed her a photo of Trenton White. "How about this guy?"

"Oh no," Martina said with certainty. "The guy who came in wasn't a ginger. I'm sure of that."

"Hang on. One more." She quickly searched online for an image of Mason McGinnis. "What about him?"

"Nope. The applicant was much younger than this guy," Martina said.

It might or might not be Johnny, but at least she knew it wasn't Mason or Trenton.

"Thank you." But as Harriet turned to go, the door suddenly swung open. She stepped back as DI McCormick and Sergeant Oduba came into the office.

"Hello, Harriet," the detective inspector said. "Fancy meeting you here."

"Quite a coincidence, isn't it?" Harriet laughed and said to Martina, "I think they're here for the same reason I was."

Martina's eyes widened, and Harriet thanked her again. Hopefully, the appearance of the police officers would speed up the process.

"By the way, thank you for that email from McGinnis," DI McCormick said as Harriet passed her on the way out. "We have the London PD on their way to talk to Trenton White now."

Harriet was pleased to hear it.

She made it to the office in time for her first of many back-to-back appointments, including an emergency X-ray and cast for a sweet German shepherd who'd gotten off her leash and been hit by a car. The dog's owner was in tears of distress that became tears of relief as Harriet reassured her that her dog would be fine.

Harriet checked her phone during a short lunch break and found a message from Jackson Russell. HEY. I'VE BEEN THINKING ABOUT YOU, AND I HAD A THOUGHT ABOUT THAT BUST OF MARCUS. ANY CHANCE YOU'RE FREE FOR COFFEE OR DINNER TONIGHT SO I CAN PICK YOUR BRAIN?

Harriet's first instinct was to refuse so he didn't get the wrong idea. But then, she'd told him she had a boyfriend, so surely he wasn't still flirting with her. She was reading too much into it.

Besides, she wanted to know what his thought about the bust was. She didn't have anything else going on tonight. Maybe she could meet him for coffee.

I HAVE SOME TIME BEFORE DINNER, she texted back. MAYBE WE COULD HAVE COFFEE AROUND 5?

COFFEE SOUNDS GREAT, he replied. SAME PLACE?

SEE YOU THERE.

She put her phone away and went back to work. By the time they were done for the day, Harriet was exhausted. She would finish cleaning up and run a brush through her hair before she had to go meet Jackson.

But as she swept the waiting room, Polly said, "So what's the latest? Do you know who's behind the thefts yet?"

"I still think it's Johnny and Riley, though I'm waiting on a few things to confirm that."

"Why? Give me the whole scoop," Polly said.

Harriet glanced at the clock. Usually, Polly was ready to leave as soon as they closed. "Don't you need to go?"

"I'm waiting for my ride. We might as well try to solve this thing in the meantime."

"Okay. You already know about the marine research center and Riley knowing all about the different kinds of art. But then there's this photo." She showed Polly the whale-watching photo on her laptop. "If you compare it to the picture of Johnny on the research center boat, they could easily be the same person. And maybe it's even the same boat. I can't tell."

"Back up." Polly pointed at the picture from the whale-watching tour. "What is this photo?"

Harriet told Polly how she'd found the picture and about her trip to the marina that morning to try to find the owner of the boat, and about how the guy in the photo could also easily be the guy pictured in the security camera footage.

"In the *what*?" Polly demanded.

"The security camera footage. Oscar sent it to me. I'm not sure he should have, but you better believe I watched it."

"I should think so. Let me see it."

Harriet brought up the footage and pressed play.

Polly watched, nodding as Oscar came in and went through the room and out, and then she gasped when, on the screen, the thief broke into the case and scooped up the coins. "That's bold. In broad daylight, with so many people around?"

"He obviously knew what he was doing, so he was efficient about it," Harriet said. "You can't tell who he is at all though."

"It *could* be the same guy from the whale-watching tour." Polly squinted at the screen. "Or not."

"I know." Harriet sighed. "I wish there was some way to know for sure."

"Agreed. Have you learned anything more about Shane O'Grady or Mason McGinnis?"

"Nothing new on Shane. No one can believe he wasn't involved, because of who he is. I have to say, that feels a bit unfair."

"You don't get the nickname Shady O'Grady for no reason," Polly pointed out. "Unfortunately, after his past behavior, he'll have to prove what he told us about turning over a new leaf."

"But I can't find any connection between him and this case, and I was inclined to believe him when he said he'd changed," Harriet said. "But Mason sent me something interesting." She pulled up the email from Mason and showed it to Polly.

"Trenton White." Polly reached over, opened a new browser window, and typed in the name.

"I already searched for him but didn't really find anything," Harriet said.

Polly fired her desk computer back up, put Trenton's name in her own search engine, and clicked through the links Harriet had seen. "He's quite posh, isn't he?"

"I suppose. Though if he's so rich, why would he need to steal art?"

"Maybe he's not as rich as he pretends to be. Maybe he's in debt. Maybe the family lost its fortune. All kinds of possibilities." She scrolled the links. "A prep-school boy. That checks out."

"It does?"

"Totally. It's not the best one though."

"Best one?"

"Sure. The one the royals go to is obviously the best. This one is not that, but it's still exclusive and expensive, of course."

Polly opened the website of the school mentioned on Trenton's social media and ran a search for his name. She found a much-younger photo of him in a uniform at a podium. The caption beneath the photo said that Trenton had been captain of the debate team.

Harriet studied the photo for a moment. There was something familiar about it. She'd never seen it before, never heard of Trenton before yesterday, but something about the photo rang a bell for her. What was it? Was it the same school Johnny had gone to?

Polly moved on, clicking through to pages about the history of the gallery Trenton worked for and the places he'd worked earlier in his career.

Meanwhile, Harriet looked up Johnny again and saw that he and Trenton hadn't gone to the same school. Whatever brain tickle was there, she couldn't resolve it now.

Polly continued to search through pages of results for Trenton White, but nothing indicated whether he might be involved in the thefts.

Harriet was still thinking about the photo of Trenton in his school uniform. She'd seen that uniform before—and recently. But where?

"Could it be him in the museum?" Polly asked. She pointed to Harriet's laptop.

"I tried to figure that out, and I couldn't tell," Harriet said.

They watched the video again, but it wasn't any clearer.

She tried to think through all the places she'd been the past few days. Where had she seen that school uniform? Who else did she know who'd gone to such a school? Liam Beresford had probably gone to a boarding school, now that she thought about it. Had she seen a similar uniform at the manor?

The door opened. Polly smiled, excited, until Riley stepped into the waiting area. Polly's disappointment was palpable. Harriet suddenly realized Polly wasn't waiting for her brother to pick her up, but someone else, and she had to smother a grin.

"Hey," Riley greeted them, all smiles. "I'm done at the gallery for the day, and I thought I'd come over to see how it's going and whether there was any update on that stolen art."

Harriet was still stuck on the uniform. Had a photo of kids in public school uniforms been used as a decoration somewhere? Was it one of the pictures on the wall at the Crow's Nest or at the coffee shop?

"Ooh, what's this?" Riley leaned forward.

Harriet realized with a start that Riley was looking at the computer screen, where the security camera video was still pulled up. Polly had paused it as the thief was putting the display case lid back in place. Harriet's instinct was to hide it—if it was Johnny on the screen, the worst thing would be for Riley to realize they were on to him.

But it was too late. She'd already seen it.

Riley's eyes widened. "That's the Atkinson, isn't it? I know that room. I've been there a bunch of times. And that's—oh my goodness!" If she was acting, she was good at it. She gasped. "This is when those coins were stolen, isn't it? And is that the thief?"

"It is," Harriet said. She watched Riley, trying to pick up on whether her surprise was genuine. If anyone would recognize Johnny, Harriet would guess it would be his girlfriend. Did Riley's lack of recognition mean it wasn't him? Or was she lying? "We're trying to figure out who it is. He's well-disguised, as you can see."

"I'll say." She leaned forward and rested her arms on the counter. "Can I see the whole video?"

Harriet glanced at Polly, who shrugged slightly. What did it matter at this point?

"Sure." Harriet restarted the video and observed Riley as the young woman watched the scene unfold on the screen.

Like a bolt of lightning, Harriet remembered where she'd seen that school uniform before.

Before she could process the realization, Riley tapped the space bar, freezing the video. "Polly, will you rewind?"

Polly backed the video up.

"There," Riley said.

Polly pressed play, and they watched the same scene play out again.

When the thief turned and headed toward the door, Riley paused the video again and pointed to the screen. "The shoes."

"What about them?" Harriet squinted, trying to see whatever it was Riley saw. They were dark shoes, but Harriet couldn't tell any more than that.

"I've seen those shoes before." Riley held her hand to her mouth. "Oh my goodness." She tapped the space bar again, and the video kept playing. "It can't be."

"Do you recognize him?" Harriet asked as dread settled into her stomach like a stone.

"I noticed the shoes at first, but I hoped I was wrong." Riley shook her head. "But when he walks away, it's obviously him. I know who that is."

And then Harriet realized that she did too.

CHAPTER TWENTY-THREE

Harriet braced herself for the words she knew were coming. She didn't know how she'd missed it. She hadn't noticed the shoes, but she'd seen them before too. And now that she knew who she was looking at, she couldn't believe she hadn't recognized the movements and mannerisms.

And Harriet felt certain that Riley hadn't known. The shock that had crossed her face was real, and she was processing her confusion and dismay at the same time Harriet was.

"It's Jackson Russell," Harriet said. "Isn't it?"

Riley nodded. "He loves those shoes."

The black trendy sneakers he wore both times she'd seen him.

"What?" Polly looked from Harriet to Riley and back again. "What about his shoes?"

"Those are Dr. Russell's shoes," Riley said. "You can kind of make out the logo on the side, and their shape is also distinctive."

"I don't know how I missed it," Harriet said.

"But how did *you* figure it out?" Polly asked Harriet. "You just told me you thought it was—" She broke off, clearly thinking better of accusing Riley's boyfriend in front of her. She tried again. "You said you didn't know who it was a few minutes ago."

"Jackson went to school with Trenton White," Harriet explained. "I knew I'd seen that uniform before. There's a photo in his office of him and his friends from school. They're all wearing those uniforms. There was a kid with bright red hair in the photo, and I think it might be Trenton. Either way, the uniform is a clear connection."

"But why would a professor—an archaeology professor, no less—be stealing ancient coins?" Polly asked.

"He knows how much they're worth," Harriet said. It was so obvious. How had she not seen it? "He gave me the book he wrote on the Norse settlements, in which he describes advising the museum on that coin display. He's an expert on the pieces, and he's familiar with the museum from a behind-the-scenes angle. He's smart enough to have figured out the flaws in the security." She rubbed her forehead as another piece clicked into place. "And he was one of the few people who would have known about the Roman bust in Liam Beresford's collection."

"Because of my paper," Riley said, shaking her head. "I can't believe it."

"And if he poked around online for other objects, he could have come across the listing for the Stone Age bowl," Polly added. "He would have been able to recognize the value."

Riley leaned against Polly's desk. "Dr. Russell? I can't believe it."

"I didn't see it either," Harriet said. "And I had coffee with him. I talked to him about this. I asked him who would have known the value of these objects." She'd been asking him about Riley, trying to find out if he thought she could have been behind the theft, when all along she should have been asking Riley about *him*.

She thought about his text earlier that morning. He knew she was trying to solve the mystery alongside the police. Did he want to get together with her to keep tabs on what she knew, and what the police knew? She couldn't believe how silly she'd been, thinking he was flirting with her when he'd been playing her the whole time.

"How did he get the art into the lobster trap?" Polly asked. "Was he working alone?"

Harriet had a moment of panic, wondering if Johnny really was involved after all. If Johnny used the marine research center's boat to get the artwork into the trap...

"He has a boat," Riley said.

"He does?" Harriet and Polly asked at the same time.

"I've heard him talk about it. He likes to take it to Cornwall for dinner when he's trying to impress a date."

Now that she mentioned it, hadn't Harriet seen a picture of a boat in Jackson's office? And he'd said his grandfather was a sailor. That was why he'd wanted to be a pirate, or a Viking.

"What kind of boat?" Harriet asked.

"I don't know. I've never seen it."

Harriet pulled up the photo of the man from the whale-watching tour. Now that she knew who it was, it was so obvious. "I wonder if this is it."

"I bet it is," Polly said.

"So what do we do now?" Riley's eyes were wide. Whatever else was going on, Harriet felt confident that Riley was not involved. Her reactions were too genuine.

"We call the police." Harriet let out a sigh. She couldn't meet up with Jackson now. There was no way she would be able to act like everything was normal, not when she knew what he'd done. She couldn't believe he'd been lying to her, using her.

Just then, her phone buzzed with a text from Jackson. AFRAID SOMETHING HAS COME UP. I NEED TO RESCHEDULE. I'LL BE IN TOUCH.

"Speak of the devil," Harriet said. "We were supposed to have coffee later, but he's canceling on me."

A bad feeling settled over her. He'd been the one to initiate the meeting in the first place. He'd wanted to see her. And now, not long after the police show up to question his friend, he bailed on her.

Harriet took a deep breath. Maybe something truly had come up, but the timing was too perfect. There was no way he could know that she'd figured out he was the thief. But if he'd been working with Trenton, and Trenton let him know the police had shown up, he may have gotten spooked.

I'M SO SORRY TO HEAR THAT. EVERYTHING OKAY? she texted back.

Three dots appeared, indicating he was typing a response, and then they went away again. And then, nothing.

She waited for a few moments, trying to convince herself everything was fine. There was no reason to panic. No reason to assume Jackson knew they'd discovered his secret. But the continuing silence from him said otherwise. She tried calling him, but it went straight to voice mail.

"Riley, do you have a way to get in touch with Jackson?" Harriet asked.

"Dr. Russell? Just by email." She checked her phone. "He has office hours right now, so he should be in his office."

"Is there a phone number for his office?"

"What, like a landline?" Riley blinked. "I have no idea."

Harriet knew something was wrong. Jackson Russell knew the police were on to him. He wouldn't sit around and wait for them to find him.

"Let's go to his office," Harriet said.

Riley stared at her. "What?"

"I want to see if he's there."

"Van's almost here," Polly said. "He texted that he's on his way."

It was good the police were responding, but if she waited until Van got there, and then explained what was going on, it could be too late. If Jackson was spooked, he would be running now.

"Polly, do you mind waiting here to show Van what we found?"

"Not at all."

"In the meantime, I'll go see if Jackson is in his office."

"I'm coming too," Riley announced.

"Not a chance," Harriet said. "This could be dangerous. It's not safe for you to come." She wasn't about to drag a university student into this.

"You won't be able to get into the building without me," Riley said. "You need a student pass to unlock the doors."

Harriet groaned. She hadn't thought about that. "Fine, let's go," she said.

She grabbed her purse and led Riley to the Land Rover. They were halfway to the university when her phone rang.

"Van is here," Polly said. "He says Officer Oduba and DI McCormick are on their way. They were talking to the London PD but are headed here now."

"What did the London police report?" Harriet asked.

"When the detectives from the London squad went to talk to Trenton White, he stonewalled them," Van said. Polly must have put the phone on speaker. "Refused to talk. In case you're wondering, that's not something we take as an indication of innocence. They brought him in for questioning and asked him what he knew about Jackson Russell and some stolen antiquities. The London chaps just finished giving Oduba and McCormick the rundown. Where are you?"

"On the way to Russell's office."

"Harriet, I don't think—"

"I was supposed to meet him for coffee," Harriet interrupted. "But he canceled on me unexpectedly. He has office hours now, so I'm going to see if he's there."

Van gave a resigned sigh. "I'm on my way. I'll be there soon."

They parked as close to the right building as possible and ran to the door. Riley used her card to swipe them in, and then they hurried up the stairs. Riley knocked on the door, but there was no answer.

Harriet tried the doorknob. It turned easily, and she pushed it open.

It was empty.

"He's supposed to be here," Riley said. "He could get in trouble if the dean knows he isn't here for office hours."

Harriet didn't have the heart to point out that Jackson was in trouble for something a lot worse than missing office hours.

Everything appeared pretty much as it had when she'd been there a few days before—the mullioned windows, the bookshelves lined with colorful spines, the rug and squashed sofa. Except for one thing. The photo of Jackson with his prep-school classmates was gone.

Was Harriet jumping to conclusions? Was the photo there somewhere, but moved to a different place? She looked around but didn't see it. "He's taken away the proof that he knows White."

"His laptop is gone too," Riley said.

Right. There was probably a lot more incriminating information on the laptop than in that one photo.

"So where did he go?" Riley asked.

"I don't know." Harriet took a deep breath. It would be all right. Even if Jackson figured out that the police were on to him, they would find him. This wasn't some devious criminal mastermind they were dealing with. This was Dr. Jackson Russell, a mild-mannered humanities professor.

One who, in retrospect, might have been having money trouble, judging by the fact that his card was declined at the coffee shop. Who was perhaps living a lifestyle above what a professor's salary should have afforded him. Who admitted he admired pirates and Vikings, neither of which were known for caring much about property-ownership rights.

But he wasn't the kind of person who was likely to do something stupid.

Although, actually, he had already done something very stupid. And now he was about to get caught. This was not good.

He'd gotten spooked, she was nearly sure of it. Trenton must have alerted him somehow, and he'd run.

But where would he go? How could he get away? Running from the police was silly on an island. Anywhere he went in the UK, the police would find him. They would simply put out an alert, and he wouldn't be allowed to fly or board a train to another country. The only way he could possibly get out of the country was by—

"He went to the marina," Harriet said as the idea formed. "He's getting his boat."

"What?" Riley said.

Harriet was already calling Polly.

"Is he there?" Polly asked.

"No, he's gone. So are his laptop and the photo that links him to White. Can you ask Van if they were able to trace that boat registration number?"

"Hang on. I'll call on the other line." She called Van and then merged the calls. "Harriet wants to know if you were able to trace that boat registration number."

"Yes," Van said. "I just got off the phone with Martina. The boat you saw in the whale-watching photo is registered to Dr. Jackson Russell. He named the boat the *Freyja*."

"Freyja is the Norse goddess of beauty and war," Harriet said. "He mentioned her in his book."

Of course Jackson's boat was named the *Freyja*. And he could be using it to try to flee. "He's going to use it to get away."

"I'll call DI McCormick," Van said.

"Tell her to send a team to the marina," Harriet said.

"It'll take some time. They'll need to get permission from base before they can dispatch a marine unit," Van said. "But they'll be there as soon as possible."

They didn't have a lot of time. If Jackson was already on his way out, would the police be able to catch him?

Then again, how far could he go? Surely a boat the size of the one in the photo she'd seen couldn't make it across the open ocean. He would need a much bigger boat to try to cross the North Sea. That was why he'd used the lobster trap in the first place, wasn't it? Because a boat that size couldn't take the stolen goods as far as they needed to go?

She decided to find out. She called Will. "How far could a small-ish boat go on one tank of gas? Like, halfway to Amsterdam? Or less?"

"What?"

"Jackson Russell is escaping," Harriet said. "I think he's on a boat headed out of the country."

"Jackson Russell? The professor?"

"And art thief, as it turns out," Harriet said. "He's getting away, and I need to know how far he can get."

"Okay." Will absorbed the news from her bizarre phone call admirably. "A small boat may be able to get him to Amsterdam, depending on its exact size. But it's more likely that he'd head south and get closer to the continent, refuel, and then cross to Belgium from there."

"So he really could escape?"

"Ideally he would need to clear customs once he got across the North Sea, but depending on where he lands, it's possible."

"In that case, we have to stop him."

"We?"

"By the time the police have what they need to give chase, he could be long gone. Do you think Kyle would let you borrow his boat again?"

"Harriet, we can't go chasing after a suspect ourselves."

"We're not going to arrest him or anything. Just keep an eye on him and let the police know which direction he goes. We don't have to get too close to him."

Will didn't say anything for a moment. She wondered what was going through his head, whether he was upset or angry or thought she was crazy. Probably all three.

Will was a man of God. A rational, sensible man, revered for his compassion and kindness, but also for his wisdom. He was not prone to making rash decisions or acting without thinking through every side of the issue first. He, of all people, would tell her this plan was utter madness.

Which was why she was so surprised when he finally said, "I'll meet you there."

CHAPTER TWENTY-FOUR

Harriet left Riley at the university—Johnny was going to pick her up—and drove to the marina. She parked in the now-familiar lot and made her way down to the dock where Kyle tied up his boat. She scanned the boats in the harbor, looking for the one she'd seen in that photo.

It was ridiculous, of course. Searching for a white boat in a sea of white boats was a fruitless endeavor. But she strained her eyes anyway for a boat racing out of the harbor or anything else that screamed *criminal trying to escape*. At first, all she could see were small crafts motoring slowly up and down the marina toward the boat launch ramp.

But wait—there was a boat tied up at the gas pump, refueling.

Harriet squinted at the port letters and numbers. It began with *WY*, for Whitby. That made sense. It was too far away and her eyesight wasn't good enough to be able to make out the digits. There was a person moving around on the deck, but from where she stood it was impossible to tell anything about him.

Too bad it was high tide. If it were low tide, the water in the marina might have been too shallow to let boats out. But it was high tide, so Jackson could be halfway to Amsterdam by now.

Where was Will? She knew he would have had to break every speed limit to get there that quickly, but if there was ever a time for a pastor to break the law...

She peered around, hoping to see his Kia pulling into the lot or the police racing toward the waterfront, but there was nothing. She thought about going to the office to tell them what was going on, but they would be closed now. What did someone do if there was an emergency? Who could she talk to?

She stared at the boat at the gas pump again. It started to pull away. As the boat turned toward the mouth of the bay, she managed to make out the name written on the back of the hull.

The *Freyja.*

She called Van. "It's him," she said as soon as Van picked up. "The *Freyja* is leaving the marina, headed out to sea."

"What?"

"I'm at the marina, and I can see it from here. The *Freya* refueled and is headed out to open water. You have to get the police boats out here now. Or the coast guard. He's about to get away."

"I'm on it." Van hung up.

Harriet watched as the *Freyja* approached the mouth of the marina. *Please, Lord, let them hurry,* she prayed. *Don't let him get away.*

"Where is he?"

Harriet whipped around as Will appeared on the dock beside her. "Goodness. You must have sped here."

"I was given strict instructions to hurry," Will said. "So I did. Kyle's fine with us using his boat. I called him on my way over." He ran down the dock and hopped aboard Kyle's boat. "Do you know where Jackson is?"

"He's headed out of the marina now," Harriet said, pointing.

"In that case, we'd better get going." Will held out his hand to help Harriet aboard then untied the ropes that held the boat to the dock, and they motored away from the pier.

Will maneuvered through the channel at the achingly slow pace boats were required to travel inside the marina. Jackson, already out in the open water, was no doubt gunning it.

Harriet called Van again, who answered on the first ring.

"Where are you now?" Van asked.

"On a boat with Will. We're going after him." The orange and white buoys that said NO WAKE bobbed in the waves that their boat kicked up.

"Harriet, do not approach that boat."

"We won't," she said. "We'll just try to follow him so we can relay his location."

"Do you see him?" Van asked.

"Not yet, but we'll be making the turn out of the marina very soon. We should see him then."

"The police boats are on their way. I've got the coast guard mustering now too. You won't be out there alone for long. Let me know when you have a visual."

At long last—or so it felt to Harriet—they made their way around the bend to open water. As soon as Will got past the breakers, he gunned it out into the North Sea. There were several boats in the area, but only one that appeared to be racing full-speed toward the south.

"That's him," she said. "We see him, Van."

"Try to keep him in your sights, but do *not* approach under any circumstances," Van said.

Harriet said they would do their best and then called out to Will, "He says to try to keep him in sight."

Will gave her a thumbs-up but kept his gaze on the water ahead of them. He was already on the radio with other boats in the area, asking them to report any sightings of the *Freyja*.

"Can you have Will announce his position on channel eight?" Van asked.

Harriet shouted to relay the message over the roar of the motor.

The radio squawked as Will communicated with the coast guard about where they were and where Jackson was in relation to them. They continued to race toward his boat, but it seemed to get smaller and smaller as it flew nearer the horizon.

Then, from somewhere behind her, Harriet heard something— the roar of a boat motor. She spun and saw a boat barreling their way.

"Is that the coast guard?" Harriet yelled.

Will glanced over his shoulder. "No. I don't know who it is." And then, a moment later, his voice rose. "Harriet, get down."

"What?"

"Get down!" he yelled. "If they're in league with Jackson, who knows what—"

Harriet dropped to the floor of the boat, bracing herself. The radio squawked, but she couldn't hear what Will or anyone else said over the roar of the engine.

Suddenly, Will burst out laughing.

"What?" Harriet cried.

"It's Shane O'Grady!" Will called, pointing to the boat as it passed them.

"What?"

"I saw him in his boat in the marina. He must have heard the talk on channel eight and raced to try to help."

Harriet lifted her head to see over the gunnel and recognized the driver in the other craft. Shane lifted his hand to wave at them.

"How can he go so fast?" she shouted.

"I'm sure the coast guard will have questions about that," Will said. "But for now, he's trying to chase down Jackson, so who cares?"

Harriet tried to wrap her mind around the idea that Shane O'Grady might be the one to catch the bad guy. Maybe he truly had turned over a new leaf. Second chances and all that. They watched as Shane zoomed past and raced toward Jackson's receding boat.

Then there was another noise behind them. It grew louder and more distinct as it caught up to them. A helicopter banked as it flew overhead and toward the other two boats.

Then, more noise behind them, higher-pitched and getting louder. Two police boats screamed past them. Kyle's boat might not be able to keep up with Jackson, but either the police or Shane would catch him soon enough. Two more boats followed close behind. Harriet caught a glimpse of the coast guard logo as they blew past.

Harriet couldn't hear what Will was saying into the radio, and she couldn't check to see if Van was still on the phone. She couldn't hear anything over the noise of the passing boats. But Will must have heard enough to know what was going on, because at some point—Harriet didn't know if it was two minutes later or twenty— he pulled back the throttle and began to slow down.

"What's happening?" she called.

Will grinned over his shoulder at her. "They caught him."

"They did?"

"They surrounded him. Shane, the police, and the coast guard boats penned him in. There was nowhere for him to go, so they boarded the boat and got him."

"And we didn't get to see it?" Harriet was rather disappointed. She was the one who had figured out Jackson's involvement and likely escape. She'd spotted his boat leaving the marina and sounded the alarm. She wished she could have seen the conclusion of her hard work.

Will's mouth fell open, as if he didn't have any idea what to say to that. But then he threw back his head and laughed. "No, I guess they didn't wait for us. It turns out accosting criminals on international waters is actually a job for the professionals."

He was right. It was probably much better that she and Will weren't anywhere near the boats when the arrest was made. At least the professor was in police custody now and would face the consequences for what he'd done. There was plenty of evidence that would prove he was guilty.

Will slowly circled the boat around and headed toward the marina. "They want us to get safely back to the dock before they bring him in."

As Will drove the boat back to the marina, Harriet thought about Jackson Russell and wondered why he'd done what he had. She supposed he would tell the police all about it in the coming weeks, and she could only speculate about his true motives, but it was hard to imagine money wasn't at the heart of it. Jackson had the knowledge and the ability to get valuable antiquities to a foreign buyer with plenty of money. She was sure he was paid well for his trouble—or would have been, if someone hadn't accidentally pulled up the wrong lobster trap and uncovered the whole scheme.

There were so many unanswered questions. Were there more artifacts in more lobster traps? Had Jackson already successfully smuggled some out of the country? How did he feel about the pieces of the nation's history—the very objects he'd built a career studying—being traded for cold hard cash? Who was the foreign buyer? She wondered where Jackson had intended to go, whether he'd simply meant to abandon his two daughters. Maybe he had no plan, just an instinct to run once he knew he'd been found out. She knew she'd probably never know the answers.

It didn't matter. The thief was caught and would likely spend some time behind bars. She and Will were safe, and if she hadn't known better, it might seem like they were merely two people out for a boat ride on a nice summer evening.

They made it back and had just tied up to the dock when the police and coast guard returned to the marina. A line of police vehicles waited on the strip of pavement beyond the docks, and Harriet watched Jackson Russell, handcuffed, being walked out of the police boat and into a waiting squad car.

Will cleaned up the boat and then helped Harriet onto the dock. The evening light had a golden cast, and water glittered in the dimming rays. The boats bobbing in the water and the lighthouse at the end of the breaker painted the perfect summer scene.

"So there's one thing I need to say before we head back," Will said.

"What's that?"

She turned to face him in time to see him drop to one knee. He held a small box in his hand. What was he—

"Harriet Bailey, there has not been one day since I met you that has been boring," Will said. "I love your quick mind and your big heart. I love how you love the Lord and live each day to serve Him. I love how you care for all of His creatures, even the weird ones, like lobsters."

Harriet couldn't help but laugh at that.

"I love that you care enough about justice that you'll put yourself in danger to right a wrong—though, if I'm honest, I wish you would do a tiny bit less of that. I love that you never let anything stop you when you're trying to solve a puzzle. And I love that you're always ready for a crazy adventure. I love you, period. I know that life with you will be one surprise after another, and I cannot wait to see what each new day brings." He opened the box to reveal a beautiful sapphire ring, sparkling in the evening light. "What I'm trying to say is, Harriet, will you marry me?"

Harriet didn't realize she was crying until her eyesight blurred. She covered her mouth with one hand, trying to recover her powers of speech.

"I hope those are happy tears," Will said.

"Yes, they are. And yes, I will marry you!" Harriet tugged him to his feet and threw her arms around his neck.

Will wrapped his arms around her and held her close for a moment, and then he pulled away a bit and gently tilted her face up to his. He kissed her softly, sweetly, and she kissed him back.

Nothing had ever felt so right.

Will smiled at her, and said, "Well, do you want the ring or not?"

Harriet laughed again, realizing that Will still held the box. She held out her hand. He took the ring out and slipped it on her finger. She admired how it shimmered in the light. "It's gorgeous."

"It was my grandmother's. It's...well, it was one of the things Dad sent from her attic. Though she really did love *Ivanhoe* too."

Harriet laughed. That was another mystery solved.

"I thought you might like it, but if you don't, we'll go shopping and get exactly what you want."

"It's perfect." She loved that this ring had a history, one that was important to Will's family—her future family.

"Now I have a question," she said, still admiring it. "Did you bring it down here on purpose to ask me after our boat ride?"

"Oh no," Will said. "I had strict instructions to get here quickly, remember? I've been carrying it around in my pocket for a while now, hoping the right moment would present itself. I had a million different plans, but none of them seemed exactly right and, well, I got tired of waiting."

Harriet remembered seeing him tap his pocket several times over the past few weeks. "This is exactly the right moment," she said, and kissed him again.

She pulled back and looked up from the ring at Will's face—eager, earnest, and filled with love. They were going to get married. What a huge difference a year could make. When she'd moved to White Church Bay, heartbroken after Dustin called off their engagement, she'd never imagined that the Lord would give her more than she could have ever dreamed. She'd thought all was lost, but God gave her a second chance.

Even when she couldn't see it, God had something better in store for her.

And she couldn't wait to see what He did next.

FROM THE AUTHOR

Dear Reader,

The idea for this book started on a summer evening, when a friend invited my family and me to join him on his boat when he went out to check his lobster traps in Cape Cod Bay. Watching him raise and lower his traps, I had the—admittedly offbeat—idea that lobster traps would be a great way to smuggle something out of the country. The traps were just sitting out there in the water, with no one guarding them, and anyone could drop something in one and leave it there for someone else to pick up. There was nothing but open water between Massachusetts and Europe. There were no security cameras, no police, no rules. Just the perfect opportunity for a crime.

Back on land, over lobster rolls made from the evening's crustacean haul, I did a little research and learned that a Yorkshire resort called Bridlington is the lobster capital of Europe. I knew then that I had the germ of an idea for this story. The editors at Guideposts—a brave bunch, there's no doubt—greenlighted my strange story idea about lobster larceny, and I was off. But what would someone be trying to smuggle?

I started doing some research about the history of the country we now know as England, and I was ashamed to discover how little I understood about the people who have called that land home over the centuries. I guess I vaguely knew there were some things from Roman times around, but I hadn't really understood they were from *that* Roman Empire, or how many centuries ago that was.

I didn't know much about the Anglo-Saxons, who moved in after the fall of the Roman Empire, or that the Norse took the land from them (Vikings!), or anything about the Normans.

And all of that came before the medieval period, with its knights and ladies and the rise of the Tudors. Fragments of so many civilizations over thousands of years of history are still being unearthed in Britain, and I decided I wanted to explore that by having artifacts from various periods in history be part of this story.

I was lucky enough to visit the United Kingdom during the writing of this book, and I loved getting to experience this fantastic place in real life. I started in London and visited the British Museum, where I saw the Elgin Marbles referenced in this book, as well as important artifacts collected from cultures all over the world on display.

Then we went to Yorkshire, where the Yorkshire Museum in York was instrumental in helping me understand the timeline of this civilization's history. The bust of Marcus Aurelius in this story is based on a real artifact in that museum's collection, though it sadly wasn't on display when I visited. They did have a lot of coins, from the Roman period and beyond, on display.

I loved visiting Whitby Abbey, the ruins of the old monastery perched on a cliff overlooking the town of Whitby. The kind people at the Whitby Lobster Hatchery helped me understand more about the fishing and lobster industries in that gorgeous town, and I saw firsthand how stunning that part of the world is.

I was able to see how incredibly beautiful the town of Robin Hood's Bay—the inspiration for our own White Church Bay—truly is. And also, how many stairs there really are there. The whole town is built on a hill, and trust me, there are so many stairs. If you ever get a chance, please do go see this magical place. Once I got over driving on the wrong side of the road, which is truly terrifying at first, I wanted to drive around those villages and farmland forever.

I loved writing this book, and I hope you enjoyed reading it.

Best wishes,
Beth Adams

ABOUT THE AUTHOR

Beth Adams lives in Brooklyn, New York, with her husband and two daughters. When she's not writing, she's trying to find time to read mysteries.

A STROLL THROUGH THE ENGLISH COUNTRYSIDE

Whitby Abbey

The ruins of Whitby Abbey stand on the headlands over the small coastal town of Whitby, visible from much of the town, haunting and beautiful and iconic, and the ruins tell a fascinating story about the people who have called this place home through the centuries.

According to English Heritage, an organization dedicated to preserving and showcasing important pieces of British history and the group that owns and runs the visitor's center at the abbey, there is evidence that this area was settled in the Bronze Age. There were likely Roman settlements here as well in the third century. After the fall of the Romans, Britain fractured into kingdoms, and the kingdom of Northumbria became one of the most powerful. In AD 627, the king of the Northumbrians converted to Christianity, and a monastery was built on this site in AD 657.

The abbey was the site of important meetings, including the Synod of Whitby, in which Christians gathered to determine when to celebrate Easter. Different traditions celebrated on different dates, and in this meeting it was decided that the Christian Church would follow the Roman calendar. They also agreed on the formula we still use to determine the date of Easter today. It's always the first Sunday after the first full moon after the first day of spring. This decision was one of many ways in which the pope's authority was established in Britain.

The monastery was abandoned at some point in the ninth century, likely as a result of the Viking raids happening around this time. By the Norman conquest in 1066, the settlements on the headlands also seem to have been deserted. But in 1078, a new abbey was established on the site, and the initial wood and stone buildings were replaced by the soaring Gothic structure whose remains still stand today. However, much of the church was destroyed when, following King Henry VIII's decision to break with the Church of Rome and start the Church of England, Henry destroyed Catholic churches throughout the country and claimed the land and riches they possessed as his own.

After the abbey was destroyed, the land around it was owned by very wealthy private citizens, and the ruins of the church were left to the elements. Weakened by the stiff wind and rain that batters the headlands, portions of the remaining structure fell in over the ensuing centuries. These days, Whitby Abbey is a tourist attraction, a fascinating historical look at the history of the British Isles and the history of Christianity.

YORKSHIRE YUMMIES

Will's Famous Waffles

This recipe makes about ten waffles, which is far more than two people need for one dinner, but they freeze well.

Ingredients:

6 tablespoons unsalted butter, plus more for waffle iron

2 cups all-purpose flour

½ tablespoon sugar

1 teaspoon baking powder

1 teaspoon salt

½ teaspoon baking soda

1 cup plain yogurt or buttermilk

1 cup whole milk

4 large eggs

Directions:

Preheat waffle iron to make sure it's piping hot.

In large bowl, whisk together dry ingredients. In separate bowl, mix wet ingredients. Stir wet ingredients into dry. Coat waffle iron with butter using pastry brush or paper towel and pour about ½ cup batter onto hot iron. Cook until brown. Eat immediately, drenched in real maple syrup.

*Read on for a sneak peek of another exciting book
in the* Mysteries of Cobble Hill Farm *series!*

Of Bats and Belfries

By Shirley Raye Redmond

Harriet Bailey's assistant, Polly Thatcher, poked her head around the office door. With a gleam in her gray eyes, she said in her most professional voice, "There's someone here to see you, Dr. Bailey. He doesn't have an appointment, but I believe you'll want to see him anyway."

Harriet felt an immediate uptick in her pulse. Will! She glanced down at the sapphire ring on her finger. Even though they were now engaged and spent a great deal of time together, she still admitted, if only to herself, that the mere mention of his name caused her heart to flutter.

However, her excitement became confusion when Polly lowered her voice to a whisper. "The young gentleman comes bearing a gift and insists on giving it to you personally."

Young gentleman? Polly wouldn't describe Will that way. Arching an eyebrow, Harriet rose from her chair. "Who is it?"

With a chuckle, Polly replied, "Randy Danby." She stepped aside to allow the eleven-year-old neighbor boy to enter.

Harriet greeted him warmly. "Hi, Randy. What have you been up to this fine Thursday morning? Are you enjoying your summer holidays?"

As usual, Randy's dark hair was tousled. He wore a forest-green T-shirt and denim shorts and sported a bandage on one skinned knee. School was out for the summer, and it was clear that the boy spent a lot of time outdoors. He was brown as a nut, and the freckles across his nose and cheeks seemed more pronounced. His mother, Doreen, often called Randy and his four siblings her young hooligans, but she loved her children fiercely.

"Nothing much." Randy shrugged his thin shoulders. "Been riding my bike mostly, running errands for Mum and Dad, and helping around the farm as usual." He looked down at what appeared to be a pile of white tissue paper in his hands. Thrusting the bundle toward Harriet, he said, "I brought you something. I hope you like it." He ducked his head, suddenly bashful.

Polly's gaze met Harriet's, the twinkle in her friend's eyes more pronounced.

"How sweet of you," Harriet said, accepting the makeshift package. "What's the occasion? It's not my birthday or Christmas or anything."

Randy stared down at his sandal-clad feet. "I saw this figurine and thought you might like to have it. You like dogs a lot, don't you?" He regarded her with a hopeful expression.

"Indeed I do," Harriet assured him as she tugged at the parcel, which was taped with more haste than skill. "I like dogs very much. Why, this appears to be a King Charles spaniel. That's one of my favorite breeds. How did you know?"

"She always says that," Polly murmured, giving Randy a wink. "All dogs are her favorite breed."

A slow flush spread beneath Randy's freckles. "Well, I just thought you'd like it," he muttered, embarrassed. "It being a dog and kind of cute and everything."

"I do like it. Very much," Harriet assured him. She studied the brown-and-white porcelain figurine. It was whimsical and, in some ways, rather primitive. There was a small hole in the base, along with what appeared to be a dab of red paint. She saw no writing or markings of any kind. Could it be antique porcelain? Or simply a reproduction? She couldn't be sure. Somehow, the little dog seemed vaguely familiar. Perhaps she'd seen similar figurines at various shops in town.

"Thank you, Randy. It's adorable." Harriet gave him a bright smile. "Where did you get it?"

The boy's shoulders stiffened as he shoved his hands into the front pockets of his shorts. His flush deepened. "I found it...around. Thought you'd like it, that's all. Must be off now. Cheerio." He dashed out the clinic door like a frightened rabbit before Harriet could press the matter further.

Polly laughed as she leaned against the doorjamb, her arms folded across her chest. "You've fully cemented your position in this town, Harriet, and no mistake."

Harriet grinned at her in return. "I'm glad to hear it. He's a good kid." She walked to the waiting room and peered through the window at Randy, who was already making his getaway on his bike. "Does this look valuable to you? It might be an antique. I hope he didn't swipe it from his family's attic or anything. He seemed reluctant to tell me where he found it." She passed the figurine to Polly. "I have a feeling I recognize it somehow, but I can't place it. Do you think it belongs to Doreen? Could Randy have taken it from their house without telling her?"

"Couldn't say," Polly admitted. "But now that you've mentioned it, it does seem familiar. I must've seen others like it somewhere or other. Can't remember where exactly." Polly handed it back to her. "You're right. It does look old."

"I'd better put it someplace safe," Harriet said. "If it does belong to Doreen, she'll want it returned in good condition. I'd hate to get Randy in trouble with his parents, but I really can't accept this if he took it without permission."

Glancing through the front window, Polly said, "There's Celia Beem with her dog, Scarlett. Right on time. The Beems are the ones who renovated the old Quill and Scroll Inn, down by the seashore. They're new in town, but they've been making friends quickly by purchasing and hiring locally."

"That's good to know, and I appreciate their commitment to feeding into the local economy. I'll see her in a moment." Harriet hurried to the kitchen, where she carefully rewrapped the porcelain dog in the tissue paper and tucked it away in a deep drawer. She'd investigate the matter later when she could have a private word with Doreen.

Randy had found the figurine, or so he'd said. But where? In his parents' attic? In someone's trash pile? Somehow, Hariet would have to convince her friend and neighbor not to be too angry with the boy, if indeed he'd taken the whimsical ornament without permission.

Harriet returned to the office to greet her newest patient—a lovely Irish setter. The dog's thirtysomething owner was petite, with strawberry-blond hair and tired blue eyes. She was rather pale, perhaps worried about the health of her pet. Still, she greeted Harriet with a shy smile. Scarlett was equally friendly, wagging her tail and fixing lively brown eyes on Harriet with interest.

"Come in and let me have a look at this gorgeous girl," Harriet said as she stroked the dog's velvety ears. "You told my receptionist that Scarlett is having skin problems?"

"Yes, and I'm at my wit's end with it," Mrs. Beem said, leading her dog into the exam room.

With Harriet's guidance, the dog bounded onto the metal examination table.

Mrs. Beem added, "I've changed her food and her shampoo, in case she's developed an allergy. I've also been careful to keep her dog bed clean. Nothing seems to help."

She told Harriet about Scarlett's paw chewing, watery eyes, sneezing, and excessive scratching while Harriet carefully examined the dog's skin.

"Based on the symptoms you're describing, I believe Scarlett has atopic dermatitis," Harriet said. "It's a chronic inflammatory skin disease associated with allergies. It's one of the more common ailments in dogs."

"But what's causing it?" Mrs. Beem asked. "Is it her food? I've already tried so many brands."

"Possibly," Harriet said. "But food allergies in dogs can be tricky to identify. Has she been having gastrointestinal issues too?"

Mrs. Beem shook her head.

"That's good," Harriet told her. "Still, let's start with assuming it is a food allergy. Believe it or not, the most common symptoms of food allergies in dogs usually show up as reactions in their skin." She went on to prescribe a regimen of tablets that would inhibit the inflammation and then administered the first dose. "She'll probably drink more water, but this medication should help clear up her skin lesions, along with a modified diet."

"Thank goodness," Mrs. Beem said.

Harriet wrote everything down, from the medication dosage and schedule to the food changes she recommended and handed the sheet to Mrs. Beem. "Let me know if this doesn't help within a couple weeks, and we'll explore next steps."

"Thank you, Doctor," the woman said. "You've been so helpful. I hate to see my Scarlett in such discomfort."

"She's a beautiful animal," Harriet replied. Scarlett was a perfect example of the breed with her flashy mahogany coat, long sinewy legs, and sweet temper. Harriet stroked the dog's neck. "And you know you're a beauty, don't you, girl? We'll have you back in the pink of health before you know it." She turned back to the dog's owner. "Don't worry, Mrs. Beem. She's going to be fine."

"Please call me Celia," she said. "All my friends do. I hope you will too."

"Then you must call me Harriet," Harriet said with a smile. "I can tell you've been worried about Scarlett, and anyone who loves animals as much as you love yours is automatically a friend of mine."

"I've not been sleeping well," Celia admitted. "But it's not Scarlett that's keeping me awake at night. It's the inn."

"Polly told me that you and your husband have renovated the old Quill and Scroll," Harriet said. "It's not easy starting a new business, or even taking over someone else's. This used to be my grandfather's veterinary clinic. He'd built a solid practice, but it took a while for me to convince his customers that they could trust me." She coaxed the dog off the table and opened the door, calling to Polly to come in with a treat.

Celia heaved a sigh. "It hasn't been easy. At first it sounded like so much fun. My husband, Freddie, and I love the location, and the inn is so quaint and historic. I truly enjoyed redecorating and planning menus, purchasing new towels and bed linens, picking out curtains and modernizing the kitchen." Her mouth pinched at the corners. "But not everything has been enjoyable."

Overhearing this last comment as she strode through the door with a dog biscuit, Polly said, "Let me guess. Fire codes, leaky roofs, structural damage, leaking drains."

"Yes, all of that. You seem to know something about renovating old buildings."

"Those things are almost a guarantee with older buildings around here. I have a friend over in Pickering who bought an old manor house and turned it into a bed-and-breakfast," Polly explained. "It proved to be quite an ordeal before all was said and done. Drafty windows, unstable chimneys—all sorts of things like that." She offered the biscuit to Scarlett, who accepted it with a happy thump of her tail.

"I hope the community has been welcoming," Harriet said. "Sometimes it can be hard to fit in at first. I'm a relative newcomer myself. I came here from the States about a year ago. But now this is home, and I can't imagine living anywhere else."

Celia's face lit up. "I thought you sounded American. And yes, everyone has been very kind and supportive too." She paused. "Well, *almost* everyone."

"Do tell," Polly insisted.

Harriet gave Polly a warning glance. Perhaps Celia didn't feel comfortable discussing the matter. Why should she take them into her confidence? After all, she barely knew them.

But Celia seemed willing to confide in them, though she did so in a low voice. "Mrs. Mackenzie hasn't been kind at all. And that's putting it nicely."

"Who is Mrs. Mackenzie?" Harriet asked.

"Nettie Mackenzie, the owner of the Pint Pot," Polly told her. "It's that old brick inn on the outskirts of town as you head toward Leeds."

Harriet had passed the place once or twice. It looked a bit ramshackle in her opinion, though it wasn't even half as old as the historic Quill and Scroll. There was a glorious purple clematis vine growing on the south side of the building that she greatly admired, but it was the only attractive thing about the place. She'd never been inside, nor did she know the owner, but she could well imagine that Nettie Mackenzie might be resentful of the competition.

"She could be upset that she's likely to lose business to you and your husband," Harriet suggested. "She's probably afraid that her customers will start patronizing your place instead."

"That's what Freddie says. But he also says she'll have to get over her resentment. We're open for business, and we plan to stay. Besides, our prices are higher, or so we've been told. Not everyone will come to us. Mrs. Mackenzie will always have regular customers who wish to pay her more modest prices."

"Unfortunately, she offers mediocre food and hard beds," Polly said. "Don't lose sleep over that, Celia. She won't warm up to you and your husband anytime soon. Nettie would rather complain about competitors than improve her own establishment, and she acts as if she has a monopoly on hospitality. She's not fond of the owners of the White Hart either, so you're not alone." The White Hart was a well-known and popular inn that featured a great restaurant open to guests and nonguests alike.

"No, thinking about her rudeness doesn't keep me up at night," Celia assured them. "It's something else entirely." She flushed a deep shade of pink.

Harriet could tell the woman was embarrassed about something. She didn't want to pry and appear intrusive—or downright nosy, as her mother would say. But she remembered how it felt to be new in town, and she'd had her aunt to talk to. Celia didn't seem to have anyone except Freddie.

And, as usual, Harriet was curious.

Polly made the decision for her. "Won't you tell us? Maybe we can help. And we're very discreet. No need to worry about that."

Celia's flush deepened. After a moment's heavy pause, she said, "It's the weird noises in the inn, beyond what could be accounted for by an old building. I mean, we have the usual creaking and settling, but this is more than that, like rattling grates and whispering voices. Frankly, I'm scared. I'm almost embarrassed to admit it, but I think—I think the old inn is haunted."

A NOTE FROM THE EDITORS

We hope you enjoyed another exciting volume in the Mysteries of Cobble Hill Farm series, published by Guideposts. For over seventy-five years, Guideposts, a nonprofit organization, has been driven by a vision of a world filled with hope. We aspire to be the voice of a trusted friend, a friend who makes you feel more hopeful and connected.

By making a purchase from Guideposts, you join our community in touching millions of lives, inspiring them to believe that all things are possible through faith, hope, and prayer. Your continued support allows us to provide uplifting resources to those in need. Whether through our communities, websites, apps, or publications, we inspire our audiences, bring them together, and comfort, uplift, entertain, and guide them. Visit us at guideposts.org to learn more.

We would love to hear from you. Write us at Guideposts, P.O. Box 5815, Harlan, Iowa 51593 or call us at (800) 932-2145. Did you love *Caught in a Trap*? Leave a review for this product on guideposts.org/shop. Your feedback helps others in our community find relevant products.

Find inspiration, find faith, find Guideposts.
Shop our best sellers and favorites at
guideposts.org/shop
Or scan the QR code to go directly to our Shop

**Loved Mysteries of Cobble Hill Farm? Check out
some other Guideposts mystery series!
Visit https://www.shopguideposts.org/fiction-books/
mystery-fiction.html for more information.**

SECRETS FROM GRANDMA'S ATTIC

Life is recorded not only in decades or years, but in events and memories that form the fabric of our being. Follow Tracy Doyle, Amy Allen, and Robin Davisson, the granddaughters of the recently deceased centenarian, Pearl Allen, as they explore the treasures found in the attic of Grandma Pearl's Victorian home, nestled near the banks of the Mississippi in Canton, Missouri. Not only do Pearl's descendants uncover a long-buried mystery at every attic exploration, they also discover their grandmother's legacy of deep, abiding faith, which has shaped and guided their family through the years. These uncovered Secrets from Grandma's Attic reveal stories of faith, redemption, and second chances that capture your heart long after you turn the last page.

History Lost and Found
The Art of Deception
Testament to a Patriot
Buttoned Up

Pearl of Great Price
Hidden Riches
Movers and Shakers
The Eye of the Cat
Refined by Fire
The Prince and the Popper
Something Shady
Duel Threat
A Royal Tea
The Heart of a Hero
Fractured Beauty
A Shadowy Past
In Its Time
Nothing Gold Can Stay
The Cameo Clue
Veiled Intentions
Turn Back the Dial
A Marathon of Kindness
A Thief in the Night
Coming Home

SAVANNAH SECRETS

Welcome to Savannah, Georgia, a picture-perfect Southern city known for its manicured parks, moss-covered oaks, and antebellum architecture. Walk down one of the cobblestone streets, and you'll come upon Magnólia Investigations. It is here where two friends have joined forces to unravel some of Savannah's deepest secrets. Tag along as clues are exposed, red herrings discarded, and thrilling surprises revealed. Find inspiration in the special bond between Meredith Bellefontaine and Julia Foley. Cheer the friends on as they listen to their hearts and rely on their faith to solve each new case that comes their way.

The Hidden Gate
A Fallen Petal
Double Trouble
Whispering Bells
Where Time Stood Still
The Weight of Years
Willful Transgressions
Season's Meetings
Southern Fried Secrets
The Greatest of These
Patterns of Deception

The Waving Girl
Beneath a Dragon Moon
Garden Variety Crimes
Meant for Good
A Bone to Pick
Honeybees & Legacies
True Grits
Sapphire Secret
Jingle Bell Heist
Buried Secrets
A Puzzle of Pearls
Facing the Facts
Resurrecting Trouble
Forever and a Day

MYSTERIES OF MARTHA'S VINEYARD

Priscilla Latham Grant has inherited a lighthouse! So with not much more than a strong will and a sore heart, the recent widow says goodbye to her lifelong Kansas home and heads to the quaint and historic island of Martha's Vineyard, Massachusetts. There, she comes face-to-face with adventures, which include her trusty canine friend, Jake, three delightful cousins she didn't know she had, and Gerald O'Bannon, a handsome Coast Guard captain—plus head-scratching mysteries that crop up with surprising regularity.

A Light in the Darkness
Like a Fish Out of Water
Adrift
Maiden of the Mist
Making Waves
Don't Rock the Boat
A Port in the Storm
Thicker Than Water
Swept Away
Bridge Over Troubled Waters
Smoke on the Water
Shifting Sands
Shark Bait

More Great Mysteries Are Waiting for Readers Like *You!*

Whistle Stop Café

"Memories of a lifetime...I loved reading this story. Could not put the book down...." —ROSE H.

Mystery and WWII historical fiction fans will love these intriguin novels where two close friends piece together clues to solve mysteries past and present. Set in the real town of Dennison, Ohi at a historic train depot where many soldiers set off for war, these stories are filled with faithful, relatable characters you'll love spending time with.

Extraordinary Women of the Bible

"This entire series is a wonderful read.... Gives you a better understanding of the Bible." —SHARON A.

Now, in these riveting stories, you can get to know the most extraordinary women of the Bible, from Rahab and Esther to Bathsheba, Ruth, and more. Each book perfectly combines biblical facts with imaginative storylines to bring these women to vivid life and lets you witness their roles in God's great plan. These stories reveal how we can find the courage and faith needed today to face life's trials and put our trust in God just as they did.

Secrets of Grandma's Attic

"I'm hooked from beginning to end. I love how faith, hope, and prayer are included...[and] the scripture references... in the book at the appropriate time each character needs help. —JACQUELINE

Take a refreshing step back in time to the real-life town of Cantor Missouri, to the late Pearl Allen's home. Hours of page-turning intrigue unfold as her granddaughters uncover family secrets and treasures in their grandma's attic. You'll love seeing how faith has helped shape Pearl's family for generations.

Printed in the United States
by Baker & Taylor Publisher Services